HIPPIE LAWYER

Plo Villere

FOREWORD

Why the title "Hippie Lawyer"? It's as obvious as Jesus Christ. For those of you who read the bible no explanation is necessary—or at least, no explanation should be necessary. For those of you who don't, just keep in mind that most everything can and may very well be or mean the exact opposite of what it seems of appears to be or mean. And if you need any further explanation, you'd best not waste your time reading this book.

CONTENTS

The main character of this book is not the author. He may be a projection of the author's thoughts of what he might want to be, or what he might hope to be, or possibly, he is a conglomeration of other young lawyers, whom the author has observed in a very short legal career.

Ralph Veauxvois' proper name is almost as exteriorly conflicting as the idea represented by The Hippie Lawyer. But as Martin Luther King, Jr. said, happiness is the harmonious blending of the contradictions that make up our lives.

CHAPTER 1

"Where did you get those glasses, Ralph?"

"At the Optometrist! Where else," replied Ralph, in a preparedly startled and determined tone. After all, Pete, these things are for seeing, aren't they?

Pete Raymond, Docket Clerk of the Civil District Court, was on for needling the lawyers. Despite his own eccentricities, he never missed an opportunity to harp at the young lawyers, many of whom initiated their careers at his desk.

But Pete Raymond wasn't the first one to question Ralph Veauxvois' glasses. And Ralph Veauxvois didn't like it too much either. As he said, "glasses are for seeing". But there was a little more to Ralph Veauxvois' glasses than the fact that they were large, wrapped completely around his eyes, looked like a jet fighter pilot's glasses, or like sunglasses without the color; or more importantly, that no one else wore glasses like them, except perhaps the hippies. As Ralph had explained to other individuals repeatedly, he bought the glasses over the objection of the man selling them.

"I want glasses that allow me to see as much as I possibly can, which won't obliterate anything my eyes can possibly capture. I don't want to miss seeing any part of the world—good or bad," he had told the man.

In a way, his glasses were almost a religion because to Ralph, the greatest problem of the world is the individual's lack of perspective. And for Ralph, at least as far as his glasses were concerned, he wasn't about to lose any perspective. It wasn't that Ralph was actually annoyed by people constantly asking him, or the fact that almost everybody asked him; to Ralph, it was more exceptional that most people did not wear glasses like his, when just as he had reminded Pete Raymond, glasses are for seeing.

Ralph could see the problem in the paper he had just filed. It was an answer in a divorce matter. Ralph, young and quite single, was being broken into the practice of law after a two year stint in the Army, by a considerable number of these divorce cases, an area quite familiar to most of the attorneys with a general civil practice in the City of New Orleans. This was the fifth or sixth divorce in which Ralph had been involved in, in a matter of three or four months, and it was leaving a rather bitter taste in his mouth. As a matter of fact, Ralph had concluded that the best way to solve the marital problems of the United States was to abolish the institution itself.

"I just can't understand it, Jim." He directed a remark to the older attorney standing in line with him at the cashier's counter. "As far as I am concerned, if marriage is like these people view it, I don't want to have any part of it! They simply make a farce of the whole thing. Instead of selling marriage licenses, they ought to license people to have children."

"Hey, hold it a second, Ralph!" retorted Jim. "I've been married for twenty-three years myself and I wouldn't change it for anything in the world. As a matter of fact, Ralph, old boy, you are getting kind of old for the institution; why, I was only twenty years old when I got married. You know it gets kind of tough to have kids when you get to be as old as you are, what with waking up in the middle of the night and changing diapers and listening to kids scream. Pretty soon you'll have to ditch the whole idea anyway."

"Wait a second, Jim! I'm only twenty-seven years old. You sound as if I ought to be taking out my burial plot. Besides, percentages being what they are, I am not so sure I even care."

A little later, down in the First city Court, the courts in which small matters under $1,000 are handled. Ralph is taking care of a few minor matters of filing, when one of the clerks beckons to him, "Hey, Ralph! Your office wants you on the telephone."

"Thanks, Mrs. Rabouin," Ralph answers, picking up the telephone. "Hello sports fans, what can I do you for?"

"Mr. Jones wasn't to speak to you," a sweet little voice announces into the telephone.

"Oh, no, what for this time?"

"I don't know, Ralph," the little voice answered. "I just know he wants to talk to you; hold on for just a second."

"Ralph?!? Get your head out of the clouds! You've done it again," a gruff voice came hurtling through the phone.

"What do you mean?" Ralph answered plaintively.

"I was double checking through the petitions that you filed this morning, when I noticed that in the first petition you left off the title of the court; in the second, you left out all the names of the defendants in the prayer, and in the last one, you left out the amount of attorney's fees – as a matter of fact, you left out the attorney's fees altogether. How do you expect this office to run?" the gruff voice said angrily through the telephone.

"Yessir, I am sorry, sir. These details really get to me. If I'm lucky, maybe one of these days I may get the ball straight. The best thing I can tell you, sir, is that I'm trying. I'll check the petitions that I filed, and make the proper corrections," replied Ralph. And in a slightly depressed tone, "Is there anything else that you need down here, sir?"

"No. That's all. When do you expect to return to the office?"

"In about fifteen minutes."

Ralph then hung up the telephone, and retorted impishly to Mrs. Rabouin, who was sitting right next to the table on which the telephone was located.

"Sometimes I believe Mr. Jones is going to have a coronary right over the telephone."

"Oh, Ralph, you really shouldn't say things like that," admonished Mrs. Rabouin, a gray-haired grandmother, laughingly.

"Oh, I don't mean to be critical," retorted Ralph. "It just seems to me, that being overly concerned with these small details is ridiculous. It's just like the army' you worry about shining your boots while you are in school – nobody worries about shining his boots in a fox hole!" Ralph mused to himself for a few moments, and then added, "But I guess he's right. Sometimes I'm amazed at what I don't realize. And I'm supposed to be a lawyer, so engrossed in detail that I never miss one. It's just that I think sometimes we lawyers have a tendency of missing the forest for the trees."

Walking back to the office with one of his fellow attorneys, Jim Glazer, a man about ten years his elder, both in years and in experience in the practice of law, the two are nearly knocked down by an oncoming vehicle.

"You know, Jim, the most amazing thing in the world to me is, that this is the worse intersection in the city and it's sitting right beneath the eyes of the Mayor, City hall and the Judges of the Civil District Court."

"You're right, Ralph," replied Jim. "You'd think with all the 'winkies' they bought for this city, that they would have put one here." They hustled across the remained of the intersection. "Well, we survived. It would have been a damn shame if we would have been killed today. It's such a nice day after such a long rotten weekend. Nothing but rain and wind. And now, the weather is bright, sunny and beautiful, and we must spend all day inside. This just isn't the life, is it Ralph?"

"I agree with you one hundred percent, Jim. I tell you; my idea of the good life would be to be a farmer in the morning and an attorney in the afternoon; that way when we w3ould have good days, at least we would be able to spend some time outside. And just think of the physical condition that we could stay in. It's not just racial imbalance we suffer from this country."

"Funny you should make such a remark, Ralph, right in the heart of our cultural business district. It's really amazing that this blighted strip should also exist right beneath the eyes of City Hall."

"I'd agree with you, Jim, but as the Germans said, 'C'est La Guerre.' Of course, we can adopt a hostile attitude. Funny thing, it would seem utterly absurd if someone were giving a speech on it or if we were reading it in a book. See you later," Ralph remarked as he and Jim parted at the entrance to Ralph's office building.

"You've got a million calls, Mr. Veauxvois," the secretary greeted Ralph as he walked into the office.

"Anything from the Pope or the President?" replied Ralph.

"But, Mr. Veauxvois, Mr. Rollins has called here three times – he says it's very urgent!"

"With Mr. Rollins, it's always an emergency!"

"But, Mr. Veauxvois, he says, he thinks we way have allowed one of his accounts to prescribe!"

"He always thinks that – just one of these days, I hope he really finds one. Not really. That son-of-a-bitch really bugs me. Anybody else important?"

"Yes, Mr. Kennedy and Mr. Thomes. Mr. Kennedy said he must have his mortgage passed by the end of the week. Mr. Thomes said you would have to call him."

"I wonder if Mr. Kennedy will be running to the Bankruptcy Court as fast as he is running to borrow this money. I'd better call Thomes immediately. I'll answer these calls – but after that, I just don't want to be bothered. I've got this brief to write for that rule coming up this Friday. The Judge wants his memorandum, so it's important and urgent. If anyone else calls, tell them I'm either in Court or at the Supreme Court Library."

"Any questions?"

"No, sir."

"Looks, Thomes, the law of this state says that, if your matrimonial domicile is in this state, the courts in this state will not recognize an out of state divorce. I know for sure that if there are any property problems or if your wife wants any alimony and child support, an out of state divorce won't do you a drop of good. The best I figure it can do for you, is save you from a bigamy charge. And I have my doubts about that too."

"But, Mr., Veauxvois, she's got the automobile and all the furniture, and she is taking half my salary and I know she's sleeping with that guy. And she always makes it difficult for me to pick up the kids. It's just rotten. The laws are crooked and so are the Judges."

"Well, I'm sorry, Mr. Thomes. I didn't write to laws. I merely represent you in attempting to get you the best deal that you can get under the law. Believe me, I've done everything I can. There's just nothing more I can do. If you want me to file another rule to reduce your alimony, if you decide to quit your second job, I'll be glad to file it. Just let me know. Goodbye, Mr. Thomes."

Ralph hung up the phone firmly. He then picked it up again and dialed Mr. Rollin's number.

"Joe's Bar and Grill," a negro man's voice drawled though the phone.

"Oh, I'm sorry, I must have the wrong number," Ralph said politely, but disgustedly hung up the telephone. "Good grief, I have more trouble dialing telephone numbers than anything else I know. I think this new line is out to get me."

Ralph hung up the phone and dialed again, and finally got Rollins on the telephone. "What have you got this time, Rollins?"

"Veauxvois, I think you blew it this time. Remember that account by the name of Adams – he bought a refrigerator – I sent that account to you almost a year ago."

"Hold it just a second, Rollins," Ralph said, as he pressed the hold button and pushed the intercom. "Joyce, please bring me the Adams file."

"But, Mr. Veauxvois, we have three Adams files! Which one do you want?"

"The one for Mr. Rollins. The guy who bought a refrigerator."

"Okay, Mr. Veauxvois."

"Rollins, I've got the file right in front of me. You just sent us this file last week. We filed suit on it the same day. I'll let you know as soon as we get judgement – or if they file an answer. I just hope this account is better than the last three you sent us. The way you bug us, you'd think we made our money selling newspapers. When these accounts are bad, Rollins, we lose at least as much money as you do. Anything else?"

"No, that's all for now, Veauxvois."

"Okay, Joyce," exclaimed Ralph, as he burst through the door from the inner office into the waiting room. The secretary's desks are located behind counters which separate the waiting room from the secretaries working area. "Here's the product of ten hours of research and four and a half hours of blood."

The structure stood in the middle of the block amongst a row of similar buildings in varying degrees of disrepair, but none resembled the condition they had once enjoyed. Ralph's want's in too bad a state, the exterior being a fairly decent white, having a porch on both the upper and lower levels, supported by three large square columns and bordered by very old, but still very beautiful (in spite of the cracked paint) wrought iron railings. The place was probably in the best repair of any building on the block simply because Ralph had insisted when he moved there, that the landlord do the necessary repairs. The landlord's immediate "What the hell does a nice your white lawyer want to live here?" reaction then had been to refuse Ralph occupancy.

Ralph had soon been able to convince the landlord that he had no particular crusade in mind; that he would be willing to perform many of the repairs himself with the landlord's economic cooperation, and especially if he were able to enlist the physical assistance of his neighbors. The landlord could hardly object. To cooperate meant the longevity of his property, so scarce a commodity in the neighborhood, and to decline would subject him to considerable legal action, the cost of which would have been prohibitive. The landlord at least had to give it a try.

Ralph had found it much more difficult than he thought to enlist the physical assistance of his neighbors. Except for one family, the other four families living in the building were negroes – they weren't exactly all families. But they all did have one thing in common: the three apartments upstairs shared one bathroom and the three apartments downstairs shared one too. And even this has an advantage over many of the families living in the area; they didn't have to walk outside to use the bathroom, and the landlord, after a good bit of prodding, had paid to put in a gas heater in each of the halls. For the windowpanes, Ralph and his neighbors installed themselves. He had even seen to it that the broken johns were repaired and that all the plumbing was operative. These major repairs had been made by the landlord, only after considerable prodding by Ralph, who, in order to obtain the needed repairs, had obligated himself to assure that the repairs would remain permanently intact for a reasonable period of time – Ralph really stuck his neck out and it had already caused him sizeable problems, the end to which was only a hope.

"What you say, gang?" Ralph yelled to the group of small negro kids playing on the steps in front of the apartment building. There were about seven kids assembled on the steps, none of whom were more than eight years old. Ralph had fallen in love with all of them, as with all small kids, who have not yet attained an age at which they can completely mess up their lives, small and cute, fresh open books with bright inquiring covers. He would often play stick ball with them in the street or bring them up to his apartment to play with his tape recorder and slide projector, and other little gadgets with which they were not usually familiar, but through which Ralph hoped he could expose them to the world into which they had little hope of being otherwise introduced.

"Come play stick ball with us, Mr. V. Please?" The group yelled back.

"Not today, kids. I've got a meeting tonight. I've got to run upstairs to eat and get ready."

'Aw, Mr. V!" they sighed in unison. "Tomorrow, promise? Tomorrow!"

"Okay, I'll try." He took off down the hall upstairs to his apartment. And he started to use the key to his door, when he realized that it was already open, a fact which caused a deeply rooted smile of happiness. As he opened the door and walked in, he saw a slender figure in a white blouse bent intently over his desk. Her short cropped black hair contrasted sharply with her light café au lait skin and very small facial features, emphasized by the large rimless wide glasses she wore and the small yellowish illumination of the desk lamp. She didn't even turn as he quietly and carefully entered the room, walking towards the desk; she didn't even move until, startled at the discovery of his presence, he bent over to give her a light kiss on the cheek.

"How was your day, babe?"

"Real exciting, Ralph. As I told you before, that Professor Blush is fabulous. He's been telling us things that I wouldn't even believer, if he didn't document them."

Christina Brown was a tall, lithe, nineteen-year-old coed at Dillard University, the beautiful private university for negroes, started by a former dean of the more well-known Tulane University, also in New Orleans. How she had come to live with Ralph, was a revelation.

Only a year before, her parents, along with her two little brothers, had been killed in an automobile accident. Her mother had been a renegade Mississippi belle, banished from her father's plantation when she decided to marry the son of one of his hired hands, with whom she had fallen in love and become pregnant with Christina. Ralph had met her after one of the lectures he had given for the New Orleans Legal Assistance Corporation, part of a series aimed at educating the poorer and younger element of the urban ghetto population about legal problems they would face every day, and in Christina's case, consumer credit. Ever since the death of her parents she had been hounded by the finance company to whom her parents were obligated for all the earthly belongings. The insurance company had already repossessed all the mortgaged goods and had been trying to coerce her into making payments on the deficiency balances, particularly the automobile which the insurance had lapsed only a week before the accident. Chris had been the beneficiary of her father's small $5,000 life insurance policy, and the greedy vicious finance company chasers preying upon the situation both for financial and physical gain, had thought they could bluff and scare her into paying off these debts. Ralph had been immediately attracted to this vital, bright and gentle girl, and had taken considerable delight in completely resolving her problems, with a bit of retaliatory harassment of his own.

In the process they had grown to be great friends. When her old negro aunt, with whom she had been living, began to suspect that more than a friendship was involved, she heightened her antagonism from an already difficult to an intolerable state. Ralph, realizing then that further adding to this situation would cause irreparable psychological harm had told Chris that their relationship would have to cease, but this had only seemed to make the situation worse. He had looked all around, even called on his closest negro friends to try and find some more suitable place for her to live. Ut on one cold and rainy night, barefooted and bruised, she had beaten on his door, crying and begging for relief. Ralph was stunned, but at such a late hour there w3as really nothing that he could do. So, he had taken her in, made her take a warm shower and put her to sleep in his own bed, while he slept on the couch that night. He hadn't planned for her to stay there any longer than the next day, but she looked desperate, and he still had not been able to find some other more suitable place. Her aunt had been correct, she and Ralph were more than friends. A strong fondness had developed.

She had truly become a part of his life. If was as if a seed had been planted in his side and she had grown out from there. He knew that every free thought was of her, and he was not unaware of the fire possible consequences of their affection.

Five months had passed since she had first come as a refuge for just the night. At first, it had been a real trauma for Ralph and for Chris too. Ralphs' Catholic upbringing had troubled him greatly. He was greatly attracted to Chris physically, and he had known that, if she stayed, maintaining their physical distance was bound to be an impossibility.

It was not as if Ralph had never known, or that he had never fallen, but he had always tried to be careful. While he had felt considerable doubt for some time about the "Anti Sex" attitude of the church so opposed to the obvious natural inclinations of human nature, he had never really subscribed to the "Playboy" materialistic philosophy that had engulfed so many of his friends. He had refused to allow his doubts about sex to completely divorce him from his church. He still felt a need for his faith.

He had cautiously abstained from becoming involved with any of the native girls in the foreign country, in which he had spent his military tour. He had not purposefully planned not to become involved, but he had made sure that if he did become involved, he would only become involved with a girl for whom he would ordinarily, in a non-military, non-foreign situation, have become involved anyway.

And now it was Chris. Living on the edge of one of the most deep rooted ghetto areas in the south, involved with a girl of mixed blood, in a state where desegregation had never really been legalized, aside from the Supreme Court decision, and was certainly not acceptable, Ralph found himself in an even more untenable situation , than had he married on of the foreign native girls.

But he could readily remember Saturday night two weeks ago, after he and Chris had attended her sorority's spring formal dance. It was not a night full of roses.

Up to this time, Ralph had tried to remain out of Chris' life as much as possible. His intention had been to give her as much economic and personal stability as he could so that she could develop into an intelligent and educated induvial, prepared to do her part to help bring balance and happiness to the world. And even this event began rather simply.

They had not planned for Ralph to escort her to the dance.

Ralph had brought her a small sewing machine and treated her to sewing lessons at one of the fine fabric shops on St. Charles Avenue, a few blocks from the apartment. Chris had made herself a beautiful formal dress, mixing the best of American and African traits. The cloth was a multi-colored intricate design. The style, a one piece full length pants-dress with broad legs, effectively disguising the fact that the dress did have legs; and in the middle was a broad belt , a half foot in width, of a single black color which blended beautifully with the dark multi-colored pattern of the dress while successfully revealing the beautiful slick figure that was hers.

And Ralph had even taken the usual precaution of arranging for one of the older women in the building to pose as Chris' aunt, when Chris' date arrived. But earlier that afternoon, Chris had received a card that her date would not be able to attend the party because of an unexpected illness in his family. She had even tried to obtain other dates with other boys that she knew at school, but with no success.

Chris had burst forth with the suggestion – it was even more than a suggestion; it was an emotional outburst of admission for her feelings toward Ralph. And it had almost resulted in the end to their situation.

As a lawyer, Ralph was completely unable to dismiss from his mind, both the great difficulties that they would encounter and the great problems that they would create for others. He knew that once he fell, he would fall hard. He knew that just such a social occasion as this, could be the turning point that could change their relationship. Chris' outburst had made it a reality.

"I'm madly in love with you, Ralph," Chris had rushed up to him sobbing. "I know that some of my militant friends could never accept us and I realize that your career may be greatly affected – but, Ralph, what difference does their opinion matter to our life!?!"

Silence pervaded the air for a brief period, which seemed to Chris to be an eternity. Ralph was startled. He had suspected her feelings; but she had done such an effective job of disguising them, that he had not really been prepared for such an outburst. For once in his life, he was truly at a loss for words – for once, he had no quick retort, no ready answer to soothe this emotionally charged young female. And worst of all, he really had no desire to do so. His thoughts, and his feelings, had so often been turned in the same direction.

"What in the world are you saying, Chris?! You must be losing your mind! It's bad enough that we go out to dinner in private occasionally, but this would be absurd. You know that you own black friends would be harder on us – and you in particular – than anyone else could possibly be. You've just got to control your emotions!" Ralph ranted, in a loud but authoritative tone, which clearly bespoke the clash between the wisdom of his words and the strength of his emotions.

"Oh, you white beast!" Chris shrieked, as she sobbed profusely in disbelief and hatred, which evidenced that she felt the hurt of betrayal by one in whom she had placed so much of her trust in life. "You're just like all the rest! Even if you do have a few sympathetic thoughts, you're too damn gutless to face up to a situation, which you created and which you know exists. If you can't face up to this, then you might as well be dead." Chris yelled while pounding her fists on his chest, finally falling into his arms sobbing.

"Yes, I know."

Silence.

After about five minutes, Chris had regained her composure, but she still started into his face with intense disbelief, almost hatred.

"Why in the world did you do that?"

"What do you mean?"

"Why did you do it that way? For that matter, why would you want to do it at all? It seemed to me that you're just hypocritically reversing one of your most infallible tenets – one, I might add, with which I wholeheartedly concur. It seems to me that you are destroying the essence of the whole thing!"

"Look! You gotta set your priorities, don't ya? Well, my little infallible tenet you're so worried about me breaking has got to set well under the much more general precedent we'll be setting by breaking it – besides you little bush headed revolutionary, I suspect that it won't take that female nature any time to literally smother new concept in its obvious advantageous aspects." Ralph was furious.

"You look, great white legal snake! You still haven't answered my question. I'm lying here in a pool of vomit, self-defecation, blood and garbage, and the first thing that springs into your beady brain is a blood test! Of course, in as much as your brain is screwed on backwards, I guess that, is not too amazing. But you know why?! And I know that didn't receive your papal blessing!”

“You’re right!”

“I really didn’t expect to even see you again.” Chris glared at Ralph accusingly.

“It’s obvious, isn’t it?”

“Sure! I just ask these piddling questions to exercise my vocal cords!”

“O.K., O.K. Well, to put it in your lingo, I’m the one who’d hooked – pardon the corny pun – but I must admit that it wasn’t easy. I was really reviled at first by the whole scene; it was as if my whole world had dropped from under. I felt that the super-smart, super-cool legal brain of the Crescent City had blown his biggest case. I didn’t think I could afford to subject myself to such a great weakness that it might bog me down in the future, that I couldn’t afford to have my balls tied to an endemic burned out hag of female flesh!”

“Get out of here! How could you…”

“You asked! Remember? Besides, I’m here. That was my initial reaction – you know my feeling on initial reactions. You also know my feeling about jumping off bridges – that was the part that was most difficult to overcome. But I realized that you had to do it – that I would have done it myself! The rest is history.”

They had gone to the party enemies. Chris had consumed White Lightning by the beer mug until she had gotten completely smashed and violently ill. Ralph had already received more than his share of snide, cruel and outright intimidating remarks from everyone else. If it hadn’t been for his most solemn vow not to return to the war zone under any circumstances, there would most certainly have been a brawl. As it was, he was lucky to be able to collect the repulsive remains of Chris, not without both verbal and physical arbs, load her into his compact foreign low-priced second-hand car, phone the judge of the Second City Court at his house, get him and his clerk out of bed, drive to the river, cross the ferry, meet both of them at the courthouse (which also served as the police station) and browbeat the judge into marrying he and Chris inspire of the absurd circumstances.

“Veauxvois – you must be some kind of lunatic! I can’t do this! She’s black and she’s drunk and you’re nuts! She’s probably not even of legal age!”

“You’re right! But her parents are dead, and her aunt disowned her, so I had her emancipated!”

To add to the festivity of the occasion, Chris was draped over a bench, occasionally moaning, occasionally vomiting, and obviously in no condition to give her legal assent.

"Veauxvois, I ought to have you locked up for kidnapping!"

"Look judge, let's cut the hysterics and get down to the reason I got you out of bed. I know you can waive all of the usual requirements, so let's get it over with!"

"Yeah, but I can't waive her stupor!"

"Look, judge. If she remains conscious tomorrow and doesn't want to be married, you can tear all the documents up and forget about it, okay! Or she can get an annulment."

"Alright, alright! I don't believe this is happening anyway."

"And I screwed you five times! And each time you regained consciousness just enough to beg me to do it again. I thought my penis was going to fall off!"

Chris tried to get off the bed. "You bastard! I'm so sore I can't even move. First you won't even admit that you love me and then you marry me in some bizarre ritual I can't even remember. But I'm glad, and I feel horrible. You're ludicrous. Why don't you beat me – at least then my emotions would match my wretched body."

"Look Chris. If you want to get out of it, you can just call the judge and he'll destroy the records."

"Get out of it? I don't want to get out of it. My spirit is in Heaven, but my flesh is in Hell. Is this what you have been telling me Martin Luther King Jr. meant it was all about? Owww!"

GRASS

"Precisely what madness prompted you to file this asinine motion, Veauxvois?"

"You don't really think it's asinine, do you Judge?"

"You damn well better believe I do, young man! If we continue to have lunatics like you fi8ling nonsense like this, New Orleans will soon be back in the Dark Ages!"

"Is that such a bad idea? I mean, don't you think it would be nice to be able to smell some freshly cut grass down here amidst all of this steel, concrete, and asphalt?"

"I get enough of that at the country club when I play golf."

"Any of our central city fellow citizens a member of your club?"

"You used to be, Veauxvois. Why did you quit?"

"To be perfectly honest, it was the smell of over-gilded death I used to sense in the clubhouse. I must admit that it was nice out on the course with all that beautiful grass, and trees, and nice breeze. People like you made the game too slow for me; that had something to do with it. But what really got to me was the smell in the clubhouse. For one thing, the complete lack of feminine scents."

"Oh, come on, Veauxvois."

"Alright. It was just the old men, all the old men using it as a refuge right before death. And even the younger guys. It was a coffin I had no desire to be nailed into quite yet. And besides, it was keeping me from all of these other asininities."

"Okay, Veauxvois, enough of your psychiatric problems. I will definitely not sign the temporary restraining order. And if I weren't required by law, I wouldn't sign this order granting you a rule for a preliminary injunction. But you can bet your sweet life I'll dismiss that thing in the three minutes if you don't provide me with some outstanding law within five days."

"Thanks Judge. Here's your law now. After you've had a chance to look at it, let me know if you need any more."

"Now I know you're mad! How do you expect me to read all this stuff? It must weigh a pound!"

"fifteen ounces. Marvelous what work these young VISTA lawyers can turn out. Tell you what judge – once I have a chance to look at it myself, I'll digest it into three pages. Okay?"

"Within five days, Mr. Veauxvois!"

"Yes, indeed, your honor."

Judge Darrell is not known for a sweet temperament. Having remained on the bench beyond his seventy-fifth birthday because of a quirk in the retirement laws, his presence in the courtroom is often an enigma to most of the young lawyers. Fortunately, so is his outright independence. A recent case is an example. You might have thought that he would have sided with a group of wealthy old doctors and financiers who were attempting to save themselves a few bucks by maintaining the same terms in their new leases of public boat launch facilities as they had in their old ones. It was obvious he could find little merit in the surreptitious attempt to cloak one owner of a $50,000,000 yacht in the rags of a distraught beggar. His answer was curt and simple. He left that if they couldn't live with the terms of the new leases, he would open it up to public bid, which he felt should probably be done anyway; his reasoning, why should a privileged few have all of the benefits of public facilities. Especially when then terms of these leases were well within the means of the average citizen. Well, Veauxvois might not have been too happy with the draw – but he realized that it could have been worse.

Back at the office, Ron Regon, the principal young VISTA volunteer lawyer responsible for the concept and legal background upon which the suit is based, was explaining to Veauxvois the historical background of the action.

"The problem is lack legal precedent in this state – I really don't understand why you insisted on suing in state court."

"Right this minute, Ron, neither do I. What I had in mind originally is to make the provisions of our new Constitution really mean something. What good does it do to have the people say in the constitution that no private business enterprise shall obstruct the public good but do nothing to prevent an instance clearly in contravention of that provision."

"Yes, but in other states they have already successfully enforced the provisions of federal law. And besides, you know they're going to say that the state legislature and not the court should write in the specifics of this constitutional decree."

"So could the City Planning Commission and the City Council by zoning it properly – there's only one slight problem: once those skyscrapers are up, who'd gonna take them down?"

"You still have not answered my question: Who's going to enforce a state law that does not exist, especially when there's a federal law that does?"

"Veauxvois! Ron! They're rolling some big piledrivers into the parking lot right this minute! What are we going to do?" cried Denise Williams, the young negro passionately-involved secretary working with the VISTA volunteers on the case.

"Those bastards!" murmured Veauxvois.

"Denise, get the rest of the girls on the phone. Call out Veauxvois' Army. Call an immediate sit-down, sitting on the piledrivers right now. Come on, Ralph, let's go," encouraged Ron. "This ought to be interesting."

Ron and Veauxvois headed directly to the large temporary parking lot across Poydras Street from City Hall and the courthouse. The parking lot stretched all the way to the construction site of the new Louisiana Superdome, the main reason the land was now very valuable. On the way, as they crossed the parking lot under the courthouse, they noticed Judge Darrell pulling off in his car. Being a Wednesday, and noon, the Judge was heading toward his usual golf game with the boys at the Country Club. He manages this consistency by scheduling cases that have already been settled on Wednesday. It gave Veauxvois a brainstorm.

"Ah, mon ami! Bon fortune! J'ai un soignee idea! When the cat is away, the mice must play. If they want to win some games, that is."

"What do you mean Ralph?"

"Darrell's gone, right?"

"Right."

"Who's the only judge that doesn't bother with lunch?"

"Aha! Good young Judge Olivier."

"C'est vrai! Allons ze!"

Judge Oliver, to Ron and Veauxvois anyway, could most easily be described as the antithesis of Judge Darrell – young, black (mulatto color, black politically), and liberal. Like any brief description, it is not perfectly accurate and generalized would be an unfair description of both men. But for the present purpose, adequate to explain the exuberance of Ralph and Ron.

"Oh, oh! Trouble's on the way. I think I'm going to start eating lunch out like the rest of my cohorts," kidded Judge Olivier, still in his roves, having recessed his court until one o'clock, for the benefit of the parties and their attorneys. He was just entering his office from the courtroom when Ron and Ralph approached.

"Ah, come on Ed. You know you just love our trash!"

"When it's for the brothers and sisters, Ralph, I usually do. But if it's another one of your hairbrained ideas to protect the general public, spare me."

"Ed, you know that what's good for the public is good for the brothers and sisters."

"Get serious, Ralph! You know it all depends on who is interpreting the public good!"

"Well, Ed baby, this is your chance. Darrell turned me down on this idea this morning because when he looked out of his window, he couldn't see any piledrivers on the parking lot. But they're out there now, baby."

"Cut out that baby stuff, Ralph. You know I don't want to get involved in this kind of case."

"I just want you to stop these bastards from getting a foothold we won't be able to displace."

"Well, I'll have to see it for myself."

Still clad in his judicial roves (through the shock inadvertence caused by the circumstances), Judge Olivier hurriedly followed Ron and Ralph into the hall, down the elevator, out through the parking lot, and across Poydras Street (a six-laned boulevard emerging as the principal New Orleans business thoroughfare both because of the new Superdome and high-rise buildings).

"Christ, Veauxvois!"

"Aw, no, Ron! How in the hell did they find out? Do you suppose Denise told them?"

"No, Veauxvois," a voice despairingly noted. The voice belonged to Bill Singer, reported for Channel 10, WXYZ-TV. "I just happened to be driving back to the studio when I noticed that two-mile-long entourage of women with little babies. It's not Mardi Gras, yet, Veauxvois, so I figured something interesting must be up. It fits in perfectly for my Roaming Reaction Reporter Program."

Judge Olivier pulled Ralph off to the side. "Good God, Ralph! These judicial jobs are usually lifetime. What are you trying to do?" he whispered frantically into Ralph's ear.

"Ed! You know I wouldn't do anything to jeopardize your career. I spent too much time and money getting you where you are. Let me see what I can do with Singer."

"Look, Bill. Judge Olivier doesn't even really know why he's out here. How about just interviewing the ladies and me?"

"You must be kidding, Veauxvois! How often do I catch a judge in his roves in a parking lot? No go, Veauxvois. What the h...!? Tom, get the camera focused over there!"

Across the way, sitting on top of the big pile driver, a few the mothers with small babies were taking off the tops of their dresses and proceeding to nurse their babies. The momentary diversion succeeded sufficiently to allow Ron to causally hustle Judge Olivier off back to his courtroom, get the TRO signed, and have a verified copy served by a Deputy Civil Sheriff on the Supervisor of the Construction team.

"Thanks, ladies! The conscience of the City has prevailed again. It's fortunate that the conscience is located so near the heart of the city."

Ten days later in Judge Darrell's court.

"Mr. Veauxvois, you may begin your case."

"Thank you, your honor. As we pointed out in our pleadings, we shall first establish the irreparable injury…"

"No, you shall not!" grumbled Judge Darrell. "We will assume that the irreparable injury is axiomatic for the purpose of argument. First you shall establish that it, the supposed irreparable harm, is a violation of the rights of the public good; secondly, you will establish the violation of public ethics; thirdly, you shall prove how the property rights of the railroads are public and restricted by considerations of public good. If you can establish points one, two, and three, I suspect that the irreparable injury …"

"Okay, your honor. Fair enough. For my first witness, I call Mr. Henderson Wright."

Mr. Wright approaches the bench, is sworn in by the clerk, and takes his seat in the witness stand. The reporter obtains his name and address, and the testimony commences.

"Mr. Wright, what is your position with the State of Louisiana?"

"I have just been appointed to head the Department of Environment and natural Resources, established by our new state Constitution."

"In that position, what are your duties and responsibilities?"

"To be perfectly honest, Counsellor, the legislature has yet to codify the responsibilities and duties of my office. As a matter of fact, yet, they have only prescribed a temporary salary and approved my appointment. I have been charged with the duty of appointing and heading an advisory committee to write the statutory act under which the office, which I will presumably head under the present governor, will operate."

"As yet, Mr. Wright, has this committee been convened?"

"Yessir."

"And have they made any determinations?"

"Yessir, they have."

"What are they?"

"Well, of course, they are rather extensive. But generally, they have determined that the powers of my office should be quite strong in protecting and improving greatly the natural environment, including all of its sensory aspects, and in making maximum use of all of the natural resources of the State of Louisiana for the benefit of all of citizens of the state."

"That sounds rather extensive. Is there any reason to believe that the legislature will want to trim that power any?"

"I'm sure that some of the legislators will want to – but, the constitutional provision, while very concise and general, is very strong. As a matter of fact, it says essentially what I just recited a few seconds ago."

"does the constitution make any provision for regulation of private business of private resources?"

"Yessir, it does. It specifically states that no private enterprise may utilize any privately owned, shall be used in contravention of the public good."

"then there would seem to be considerable reason to believe that your office would be interested in the use to which the ground adjacent to the new Louisiana Superdome is to be made?"

"Very definitely."

"If you honor please," spoke Mr. Lionel Bevey, one of the leading members of the New Orleans and Louisiana Bars, as well known social figure, and senior partner (more than adequately accompanied this date and occasion by three eager junior partners) in the third largest and one of the most prestigious law firms in the city. "I have managed to overcome my rather strong inclinations to object, not only to this line of questioning, but also to the witness himself. As he pointed out himself, the legislature has yet to establish its will. It seems to me, your honor, that this testimony alone would be enough to sustain our objections of no right an no cause of action. It seems to me, your honor, that any further testimony from this witness will be even more irrelevant."

"On the contrary, your honor. Had the esteemed Mr. Bevey read our pleadings carefully, he would have noticed that we are only requesting a preliminary injunction pending establishment of the statues and the administrative procedures which we have every reason to believe will probably be established by the Louisiana legislature within the next six months to a year."

"This is perfectly absurd, your honor. It is unheard of. How could you possibly consider granting an injunction without basis, on a mere hope? Absolutely preposterous!"

"Oh, I don't know Mr. Bevey. I will overrule the objection. Proceed Mr. Veauxvois, but do not lead us too far afield. I will be satisfied with a clear statement of intent."

"Thank you, your honor. Now, Mr. Wright. Is it likely that your office will be interested in the ground adjacent to the Superdome?"

"The Constitution is quite specific about that, Mr. Veauxvois. No interest can be higher than that of the public good."

"Objection, your honor. This testimony is not only irrelevant, but immaterial. The cornerstone of this country is the ownership of private property – that is established in the Constitution of the United States of America."

"Thank you for the history lesson, Mr. Bevey. I am, sir, reasonable well acquainted with our Constitution. Kindly restrain yourself from insinuating my ignorance. Objection overruled."

"Continue, please, Mr. Wright."

"Yes, Mr. Veauxvois. As I was saying, we will undoubtedly be interested in the usage of that land. In this instance, I have been advised…"

"Objection – hearsay."

"Your honor, Mr. Wright's statement will merely lay a ground for the testimony of the next witness who will elaborate and stablish the second point which you have required that we establish."

"Your objection will be referred to the merits, Mr. Bevey."

"But, your honor…"

"That will be enough Mr. Bevey! Proceed, Mr. Veauxvois."

"Thank you, your honor. Mr. Wright."

"Again, as I was saying, I have been advised that there is substantial evidence of wrongdoing, specifically collusion among individuals working on the Superdome project who had privy to what is called insider information. That is not, of course, specifically my concern; that is the concern of the Commission on Governmental Ethics. But the new State Code of Ethics does contain a provision that violations may be enforced though any agency of the state government, including my office, the court, etc."

"What type of action would you contemplate being able to take?"

"Well, Mr. Veauxvois, the remedies and penalties are still under consideration, but it has been suggested that under circumstances such as have been indicated to me, my office would be able to declare the site a public resource, any profit that might be attributable to the presence of the Superdome would be deducted from the price of an expropriation which would be initiated by my office' an alternative plan which seems quite a bit harsher would be to allow my office to simply zone the property out of any usage, except a park, for example."

"Mr. Wright?"

"Yes, your honor?"

"these remedies sound extraordinary to me. At first blush they appear to border on unconstitutional."

"Ah, your honor, I am quite happy that you finally see my point."

"Yes, yes, Mr. Bevey. Please be still."

"Your honor, may I remind the court that these are only proposals. Certainly, the concept of expropriation is not unconstitutional and since when is forfeiting unfair profit such an unusual remedy – we forfeit interest when it's usurious and put people in jail who use insider information in securities violations. Mr. Bevey's people get when they are rezoning for their special advantage."

"Yes, Veauxvois, yes, it sounds reasonable."

"And, besides, your honor, I believe you will agree that with the present statement in the Constitution with regard to the environment and natural resources, we need only prove a reasonable probability that the state will take action consistent with our petition."

"Ridiculous, Judge Darrel. When we start making judicial decisions based on reasonable probability, our court system will be useless! Mr. Veauxvois' petition and his proposition are outrageous!"

"I regret to inform Mr. Bevey that I do not agree. As a matter of fact, I might very well envision granting a permanent injunction based on the environmental provision in the new state constitution, if he would prefer to avoid these outrageous probable administrative remedies to which he so violently objects."

"I beg your honor's pardon, but I would appreciate my objection being perpetuated to the remaining testimony following this line of logic."

"You have my pardon, Mr. Bevey, and your objection will be perpetuated."

"Thank you, your honor."

"Your honor, may I assume that, for the present, you are satisfied with Mr. Wright's testimony as being adequate substantiation for your point number one?"

"Yes, Mr. Veauxvois. Please proceed with your cross examination, Mr. Bevey, if you will."

"No, your honor. We would prefer to reserve our right to question this witness until later."

"Very well, Mr. Bevey. Mr. Veauxvois, proceed with your next witness."

"Thank you, your honor. I now call Mr. Ralph Redan."

After the preliminary information and swearing finish.

"Mr. Redan, what is your position with the State of Louisiana?"

"I am Chairman of the Commission on Governmental Ethics."

"Would you please tell the court if you, that is, the commission, is presently considering any action pertaining to the property adjacent to the Superdome?"

"Yessir, that is correct. We are."

"Would you kindly inform the court of the basic facts pertaining to this matter?"

"you understand that we would prefer not to go into elaborate detail in as much as the matter is still under investigation."

"We understand, Mr. Redan."

"Thank you, your honor."

"A considerable body of information has been brought to the attention of the Commission which strongly indicates that the present owners of the property acquired…"

"Objection, your honor. My clients are being publicly slandered."

"Would you prefer to concede the point Mr. Bevey and save the court some much appreciated time?"

"Alright, your honor, for the purpose of argument, we will concede."

"Thank you, Mr. Bevey."

"Besides, your honor, I cannot conceive of how Mr. Veauxvois can possibly prove his third point anyway."

"Nor I, Mr. Bevey. But we shall give him the opportunity. Please proceed, Mr. Veauxvois."

"Yes, your honor. Thank you. For my next witness, I would like to call Dr. Sergio Lonatelli."

"No, Dr. Lonatelli, kindly apprise the court of your professional qualifications."

"Well, Mr. Veauxvois, I received my master's degree in biochemistry from Tulane – my bachelor's degree is from the University of Southwestern Louisiana in botany. I received my doctorate from Johns Hopkins University in Botanical Medical Research. In particular, my dissertation was based on an experiment under controlled conditions of the balance between grass and other greenery and covered soil, that is ground covered by cement, streets, buildings, etc. and its effect on the quality of the atmosphere and the air we breathe."

"Good, God! Forgive me, Dr. Lonatelli, but your honor Mr. Veauxvois is not proposing…"

"Yes, Mr. Bevey, I most certainly am."

"What are you proposing, Mr. Veauxvois?"

"Your honor, we will show from the testimony of this expert witness that any other use of this property than just plain old grass will be highly detrimental to the health and welfare of the citizens of New Orleans, and particularly, the residents of Central City."

"Mr. Bevey, do you accept the witness as an expert for the purpose proposed by Mr. Veauxvois?"

"Your honor, I would like to ask the witness a few questions."

"Very well, Mr. Bevey."

"Dr. Lonatelli, under which gentleman did you earn your doctorate?"

"Gentleman? My principal advisor was Dr. Mary Rankins, who happens to be the foremost expert of atmospheric biological analysis in this country. She has written seven books on the subject, and her techniques are presently used in treating burn patients – you know, the air suspension system. Believe me, you don't just use any air."

"Yes, yes, doctor. Please. Your other advisors."

"Well, Dr. Ossie Ralston. Need I elaborate on his expertise in the area of cancer? Perhaps you have read his most recent popular book, Air and Cancer."

"Your honor, I submit that this witness is highly questionable. Both of the two named advisors are known to be extremists, not at all widely accepted by the general body of the medical profession."

"Mr. Bevey, I am not interested in the general body of the medical profession at this time; Dr. Lonatelli and Mr. Veauxvois, am I to understand that the doctor's testimony will mainly be drawn from the experiment upon which his dissertation was based?"

"Yes, your honor, that is correct."

"The expert is accepted by the court. The objection will be referred to the merits. Proceed, Mr. Veauxvois."

"Dr. Lonatelli, would you explain to the court the basic nature of the experiments?"

"Well, the basic purpose of the experiments was to test the medical effect of the atmosphere on the populace. Numerous animals were used including mice, dogs, cats, and monkeys. The only basic variables were greenery, particularly grass and trees, and hard covering of ground, including cement, asphalt, shells, and steel. The cubic area was, of course, exceedingly important because the amount of carbon dioxide varies to a large extent on the congestion of animals in an area. The only other basic factors introduced were highly prevalent gaseous elements such as carbon monoxide as exuded by automobiles."

"Doctor, what were your basic empirical findings?"

"Many of the findings, of course, were to be expected. For example, when the amount of carbon monoxide is considerable, say the percentage present at rush hour in any large central city area, the degree of toxicity is high. What may be of concern to you in this matter is the situation noted above when the amount of grass and greenery is increased. The main and most interesting factor is saturation. Under what we set as normal circumstances for a downtown metropolitan area, precisely the same situation where there are large buildings and streets and very little greenery with a large concentration of animals, the toxicity factor is overwhelming. As a matter of fact, prolonged exposure clearly leads to an abnormal incidence of cancer of the throat, lungs and skin, considerable high blood pressure, and disease related insanity."

"Objection, your honor. This testimony is so sweeping and so unsubstantiated."

"Mr. Bevey, I would appreciate you holding your breath for a few more minutes at least; from what the doctor says, it may be some of the last you get."

"Excuse me your honor."

"Excuse me too, Mr. Bevey. Please continue doctor."

"We cannot give you a detailed analysis of many of these results. For example, we cannot tell you why there was a much higher incidence of disease related to the balance or imbalance of the factors in the test – merely that the evidence was higher when only these variables were changed. And, even more important, the incidence of these diseases under what we now consider to be "normal" circumstances is very markedly reduced by weighing the variables heavily with greenery as opposed to sell covering substances such as concrete, asphalt, etc. What this means in practical medical terms is quite simple. Those who only work or spend eight hours or so in the center city may not be noticeably affected by this imbalance but may very well be markedly enhanced by the favorable greenery weighting. And, most importantly, those who live, we often refer to it as "being trapped" in the inner city, and who are noticeably affected in an adverse manner by the unfavorable weighting are also conversely inclined to be "cured" by the favorable weighting much like a longtime smoker who not only kicks the habit but also does deep breathing exercises to clear his lungs and rejuvenate his circulatory systems."

"Thank you, doctor. Mr. Bevey, do you have any questions of the witness?"

"Yes, your honor."

"Proceed, Mr. Bevey."

"Doctor, on what animals were these tests run?"

"The first test was run on white rats. Then, on dogs. Then on chimps. And finally, on humans."

"How many humans?"

"Twenty-three hundred and forty-two."

"Winos and welfare mothers?"

"Excuse me, sir, but your insinuation is a professional insult. If we did what you suggest, how would I be able to make an assertion regarding the difference between those who are only exposed for eight hours and those who are continually exposed. Naturally, the humans were a representative sample. Or perhaps you are suggesting that every businessman like yourself is a wino sir."

"I am sorry, sir. Forgive me. Your results simply strike me as absurd."

"Not absurd, sir – unexpected. The situation which led to our experiments came about over such a long period and include what appear to be so many diverse factors, that as obvious as they really are, like the forest and the trees, we are often least capable of perceiving the most obvious."

"Is it not possible, Doctor, that the results of the experiment, conducted under laboratory conditions, may turn out to be inaccurate under actual living conditions."

"Yes, it is possible. However, we have already received preliminary reports from other institutions and agencies on the normal checking out any scientific report as radical in its results as this one is, and so far, they all tent to indicate that very little adjustment will be necessary."

"That is all I have, your honor."

"Thank you, Doctor. Veauxvois, do you have any other witnesses on this point?"

"Not unless you feel that the evidence presented thus far, is inadequate, your honor."

"Veauxvois, you, not I, are trying this case; however, the Court does not wish to be overwhelmed by unnecessary testimony. After all, this hearing is only for the purpose of a preliminary injunction for a specific and limited time. Mr. Bevey, do you have any testimony of equal strength to rebut the doctor's testimony? I do not, or course, Mr. Bevey, mean a few "in house" doctors who will merely mouth, at your promptings, discrediting statements which have not been firmly established by experimental or scientific or clinical data which would directly and clearly contradict the evidence thus far presented."

"As you can imagine, the testimony presented today was quite surprising, to say the least. I now have two of my assistants researching the point. We would appreciate a recess until tomorrow to complete our work on this point."

"I am sorry, Mr. Bevey. You have adequate resources to research the point without a recess. Besides, I find it impossible to believe that you have not thoroughly researched this point already Mr. Bevey."

"Thank you for the compliment, your honor, but…"

"Mr. Bevey, we shall continue to the next point immediately. If we finish today, and I am inclined to grant the injunction, I will mark the record submitted until tomorrow."

"Thank you, your honor."

"Veauxvois, will you kindly proceed to the next point."

"Your honor, I now call on Mr. Bevey to produce the names and addresses of the parties involved in The Little Red School House Trust including a recorded copy of the Trust instrument, as called for in my subpoena duces tecum."

"Your honor, I object. No foundation has been stablished for any such requirement. Under what authority can such a subpoena be served on me as attorney for the plaintiff? And under what authority must I produce such records, assuming I have them?"

"A law, Mr. Bevey, which says that Trust instruments must be regarded."

"Under what penalty, Veauxvois?"

"Contempt, Mr. Bevey."

"Why, your honor?"

"If Mr. Veauxvois can establish that the land which is the point of this suit is owned by a trust called The Little Red School House and you and the Notary Public, who handled the purchase, I will require you, under penalty of contempt, to produce the Trust instrument and provide the names of the principals."

"Your honor?"

"Yes, Mr. Veauxvois?"

"I have here a verified copy of the Act of Sale which I offer in evidence as F…"

"Your honor?"

"Yes, Mr. Bevey?"

"We will consent to the judgement as prayed."

"Did I hear you correctly, Mr. Bevey?"

"Yes, you did, your honor."

"May I ask why, Mr. Bevey?"

"No, you may not, Mr. Veauxvois! Count your blessings and do not ask any more of me than you do of God."

"The clerk will draw the judgment."

"Thank you, your honor."

"You are welcomed, Mr. Veauxvois."

"Great work, Ralph."

"Hell, Ron, we haven't won the ballgame, but at least we're ahead at the end of the first inning. But I must admit I'd rather protect a lead than hold down a margin of loss."

THE CEREMONY

"Now!"

"Now?"

"Yes, right now!"

"Today?"

"Yes!"

"But…"

"But what?"

"I just think it might not be possible to arrange it today."

"Why not?"

"Well, for one thing, they may not wish to rush something like this – they do not, if you didn't know it, particularly like the manner in which we have proceeded so far."

"Does that mean that you are not going to try?"

"Do I ever fail to try?"

"No, not usually."

Ralph picks up the telephone and dials. "Hello, Tom?"

"Yes, is that you Ralph? How are you?" the voice on the other end answers.

"I know tomorrow's your big workday, but I wonder if you could do me a favor today?"

"I'll try if I can."

"Chris wants to bless it today, tonight that is, just before midnight. Then…" Ralph continues with all of the detailed requirements she has made for the ceremony.

"Man, Ralph, that's heavy stuff. What are ya trying to do – get me defrocked?"

"I don't understand, Tom? There's nothing morally wrong with the act itself. He created it, didn't he? So, what's the problem?"

"You know full well what the problem is. Your basic logic, excluding the human factors involved, may not be perfect, but I must admit I can't flaw the basics."

"Look. If the place is securely locked from the outside, and Father O'Malley knows that we don't want any interference under any circumstances and that the ceremony will last until daybreak, what kind of problems can there be. There's not going to be any loud or disturbing music. And no people."

"Okay, Ralph, I'll try. I'll be back with you in a few minutes."

"Thanks, Tom. I really appreciate it."

"Don't worry, I'll remember, ol' buddy."

At five minutes to midnight, Ralph, Tom, two tall young black men dressed in dashiki's, and the woman, barefooted and covered only by a lace black mantilla so large that it trailed on the floor enter the large St. John's Catholic Church illuminated only but the altar's candles glistening off the beautiful gold brocade on the church pillars, candle holders, and statues on the altar. The modern bronze crucifix loomed almost like an apparition over the entire area. The two young black men approach the altar first and sit to each side of it on the floor, legs crossed. Tom then approaches the altar dressed in his all black vestments. The two young men then proceed to play in strange soft tones, one on a handmade flute and the other on small drums also of native design, mysterious sounding tunes of mixed voodoo and African origin. Ralph approaches from the side carrying a large container of wine and one of water. And then, up the center aisle carrying one large loaf of French shaped, but brownish-black colored bread, the woman danced toward the altar, the mantilla waving lustily with each movement of her madly gyrating hips and legs, head snapping proudly and defiantly from side to side, front and back, in perfect time with the music. As she reaches the altar, she hands the loaf to Tom, and crouches in a heap immediately in front of the altar. Ralph approaches, hands Tom the water and wine, and joins her in a crouch, his dashiki covering completely his otherwise unclothed body.

"I am the Way, and the Truth, and the Life. Whosoever believeth in Me shall never die, but shall live unto life everlasting…

"In my father's house, there are many mansions. Now, I am going there to prepare one for each one of you…"

"Do you, Miss, agree to dedicate and commit yourself completely to the life and happiness of Ralph Veauxvois."

In mumbled and almost too softly to be heard voice, she answers," Yes, I do."

"Do you, Ralph, completely dedicate yourself to the life and happiness of this woman?"

Strongly, Ralph answers, "Yes, I do."

"By the power invested in me by Holy Mother the Church, as a representative of the God of us all, I remind you that and I hereby join you both together and henceforth you are of one flesh."

Tom continues to consecrate the bread and wine. He, and the two young black men partake small portions of each and then quietly leave the church. The two young men remain, one at each entrance.

As soon as the lock on the door is heard to latch, the woman rises, disrobes from her mantilla, and spreads it over the altar, removing the bread and wine and placing them on the floor. Ralph then rises, removes his dashiki and places it on the altar, and sits down next to her. She breaks the bread, keeps half, and hands half to Ralph. They both eat and drink from both the wine and water jugs. After finishing a little, they stop, embrace and dance softly around the sanctuary, the woman running her long soft fingers up and down his spine. He fondly touches her small buttocks, hips, and ribs. Both become more and more feverishly attracted, bumping and grinding to a beat they obviously both feel, and the, toward the altar, he lifts her up. She stands on the altar as he climbs after her, laying down on his back, fully excited and extended, as she presses her pelvis onto him and begins to work feverishly up and down. She pushes onto him, harder and harder, whispering softly, "Deeper, deeper," over and over as they both pant in the silent room. He thrusts into her violently at her every thrust, sweat pouring down their bodies and they kiss vigorously, grasping each other in a tight embrace, exploring each other's mouths with their tongues as they reach the climax. She lays atop him, softly whispering, "One flesh, one flesh…"

The ritual continued in the same manner, with brief rests, until the early morning light when they gathered her mantilla, his dashiki, the wine and water jug, and quietly left the church and were driven off by the two young black men.

CRIMINAL PRODUCTION

"Look, Tony. I want you to get the hell out of here. You understand, Mrs. Smith? This kid has got to get super-underground and way the hell out of here."

"Yes, Mr. Veauxvois. We understand, don't we Tony."

"Yea, Ralph baby, I dig."

Later at the police station.

"Veauxvois, you knew that kid was going to take off. You probably helped him. You ought to be behind bars yourself. It's liberal jackasses like you that keep this country in trouble. If those kids were permanently removed from the streets, they would be safe for everyone. It's an absolute disgrace and so are you."

"I appreciate your perception, Captain Dugan. It's sympathetic and concerned peace officers like you upon which the citizens must rely. God, are they in trouble?"

"Look, Veauxvois, if you give me any more trouble…"

"Captain, you were the one who sent the squad car to deliver your personal "invitation" to join you at this impromptu witch hunt. I have no idea where Tony Smith is. Would you like to have me take his place?"

"That's probably not a bad idea. At least that would get you off the street."

"I would love to accommodate you Captain. But Judge Christman has invited me to his little party Monday morning at nine a.m. His, like yours has been, is mandatory. I just hope that he is more courteous than you."

"Get out of here Veauxvois."

"Are you providing transportation?"

"Hell, no."

"You mean you're going to subject me to walking in Little Africa? Or maybe you should be concerned that I might molest the populace."

"Outta here, Veauxvois."

Inside the courtroom of Judge Christman, in the federal district court located in the "new" Courthouse on Royal Street in the French Quarter, "Here ye, here ye, here ye, Section 'A' of the United States District Court for the Eastern District of Louisiana, New Orleans Division, is now in session. The honorable Judge Horace Christman presiding; be seated and no smoking."

After handling several preliminary and summary matters, Judge Christman asks, "Are we prepared to proceed with Mrs. Regina Smith et al vs. the State of Louisiana?"

"Yes, your honor. The helicopter is waiting for us on top of the building."

"Who will accompany us?"

"It will be just you, your honor, Mr. Tompkins, and myself. We will be met there by Mr. Aucoin of the Department of Corrections."

Scotlandville is a nice sounding name for a little town. If you were told that your child was being given a free summer vacation there, off-hand, you would not necessarily be concerned except if you know that Scotlandville is the little town near the state capital where the most serious juvenile offenders are incarcerated. And not a particularly attractive institution.

"Where would you like to start the grand tour, your honor?"

"I will leave that up to you, Mr. Aucoin. But I must warn you that I expect to be shown the entire facility. And I want to see it in its usual operating condition."

"Don't worry, Judge. The only way they could possibly have changed the situation would have been to destroy it and rebuild it in three days. And as far as I know, Christ hasn't returned to the Earth yet."

"They only give us $1.50 per child per day to run this place, your honor."

"What do you mean they, Mr. Aucoin. Aren't you in charge of the budget for all of the juvenile correctional institutions in this state?"

"Yessir. Well, I mean sir, I administer what the Board of Corrections actually has the power to set policy over."

"Who prepares the budget?"

"Well, I do."

"How much do you allocate to the other two facilities?"

"Which facilities, your honor?"

"Is this the only juvenile correctional institution in this state, Mr.

Aucoin? Do you mean to tell me that the only children who are incarcerated for crimes against the state are black? That's all I have seen around here."

"Well, ah, yessir. There are two other facilities."

"And?"

"And, what, your honor?"

"How much per child is allocated at the institutions?"

"$8.50 and $9.50."

"Good, God, man! Do you mean to tell me that young boys must sleep in a place like this? It looks like the inside of an abandoned gymnasium locker room toilet area – and it smells that way too!"

"No, your honor, this is one of the girls' rooms."

"Where do they dress and where do they keep their clothes?"

"Here."

"What do you mean here. I don't see anything that resembles a private place to dress and I do not see any clothes."

"Well, they don't come here for a social event. And, besides, these kids don't have much anyway."

"Is that the way it is at the other institutions?"

"It most certainly is not, your honor. Here, look at these pictures. The $8.50 is the amount they spend on the white boys – and $9.50 is for the white girls. They each have separate institutions each larger than this facility with one third the kids. As you can see, the other institutions look like eastern boarding schools compared to this place," shrieked Veauxvois.

"Is that correct, Mr. Aucoin?"

"Well, your honor, I wouldn't say that."

"You mean the other places are as bad as this. Do any of these toilets work? How many kids live here?"

"As of today, 986."

"Tompkins, I have seen quite enough. Veauxvois, you will prepare an order integrating all the facilities immediately, distributing the children uniformly among the facilities, and directing the use of funds to be evenly distributed to the benefit of each child equally. Give them on month to implement it."

"But, your honor, this will cause chaos. God well never be able to do it. It will be a disaster."

"Are you trying to tell me that these black kids asked to come here, and the white kids were the only ones required to attend. Or perhaps you think we should maintain them all in the way they are accustomed."

"No, your honor. But the mixture is going to be like mixing two explosive substances."

"It may be what we need, your honor. Maybe if these places blew up the public might recognize this place is worse than a malaria factory.

Perhaps you might ask Mr. Aucoin where the educational and correctional facilities are?!"

"Well, Mr. Aucoin."

"We have tried, your honor. These kids are uneducable. There are just too many of them."

"You mean to tell me that this is supposed to be a classroom."

"They just break the place up, your honor."

"Add to your order Veauxvois that each child at these facilities is to be tested and placed at the proper class level. Adequate teachers are no greater than the ratio in our regular public schools of pupil to teacher. Additionally, the Public Affairs Research Council is to be directed to prepare a plan for Vocational Education and Special Education. Those children who are retarded are to be separated for the Special Education classes. The State will pay the cost of the PAR study which will be implemented immediately upon completion. Is that clear Veauxvois?"

"Yes, your honor."

"Tompkins?"

"Yes, your honor?"

"May I tell you, Mr. Aucoin, that I am sufficiently irritated to want to hold you in contempt immediately. When I return, I had better not recognize this place. And you had best relay my ire to the board. This place is an absolute disgrace. If someone had set out to design a plant to produce criminals, they could not have done a better job. Let's get back to New Orleans.

The copter made its way onto the lawn of the scenic old Royal Street courthouse with Captain Dugan looking on from the front seat of his patrol car parked in front of the building.

As the judge and Veauxvois debarked and parted ways, the judge into the courthouse and Veauxvois down the street, Dugan drew up alongside Ralph and called him over to the car.

"What can I do for you Dugan?"

"Got something for you on that juvenile case. Hop in."

His mind still preoccupied with the judgement which the judge had directed him to, Ralph obediently obliged. When they arrived at the police headquarters, and after they had entered the booking area, Dugan informed Ralph that he was under arrest for aiding and abetting an escape, the escape of the juvenile offender.

"You have got to be out of your mind Dugan! If Judge Christman knew of this, your ass would be in jail immediately for contempt and for obstructing justice."

"That Veauxvois, is your problem. Not mine. Now you can give the Sergeant your valuables and join the other criminals in their cells."

"Dugan, I've got to get that judgement ready for tomorrow morning. I really don't have time to play games."

"You're always bitching about the jails, Veauxvois. Now's your time to check one out firsthand."

"inasmuch as you didn't bother to read me my rights, I assume you will at least let me call someone."

"But of course, Veauxvois."

Ralph dialed his office. "Ron, Dugan's got me locked up over here at Central Lockup. Get the girls working on the judgement – just follow the prayer to the letter – you said it, the judge was horrified – and try to find somebody for RQR."

After he hung up, he proceeded with the Sergeant to a small, but clean quarters in the House of Detention. Run by the police department for arrested individuals and those charged and sentenced with minor municipal offenses, the House is a relatively nice place to spend confinement.

About an hour later, "Okay, Veauxvois, they're waiting for you downstairs."

When Ralph got down to the desk, but was still behind the big iron bar door, Ron was beside himself with laughter. "Man, if ever there was a guy who looked the part, you're it Ralph. Your clients must be rubbing off on you."

"You mean I look like a ten-year-old kid, a babe in arms?"

"Not exactly, Ralph."

"Tomorrow at 9am, Mr. Veauxvois."

"Sergeant, I must be in federal court at ten tomorrow."

"Mr. Veauxvois, you know I don't set policy."

"Okay, okay."

Back at the office, "Everything looks okay, Ron. Redistribution of the kids on a fully integrated basis among all the three institutions; equal distribution of funds on per capita basis. Looks fine, Ron. Better grab a bite and hit the rack. You will have to convey my apologies to Judge Christman tomorrow morning. Let me know how it goes."

The next morning in Criminal District Court.

"Here ye, here ye…Next, Ralph Veauxvois – Please step forward!"

"Mr. Veauxvois, what in the world are you doing here?"

"I do not know, judge. Perhaps you can enlighten me?"

"It says that you are guilty of aiding and abetting the flight from justice of a juvenile offender. Is this correct?"

"If you mean how do I plead? Not guilty."

"Mr. Prosecutor, what is your recommendation as to bail?"

"First offence. $500."

"Do you have bail, Veauxvois?"

"No, your honor. I do not wish to post bail."

"Well, that is unnecessary in your case, Mr. Veauxvois. Being a member of the bar, and this appearing to be a rather exceptional case, I will release you on your own recognizance."

"No thank you, your honor. I see no reason why I should be given any preference over these poor victims of society who never even had the chance to get an education or a place in society. Besides, now is as good a time as any to complete my inspection of prisons."

"Veauxvois, I will not allow this!"

"Why not? Whose constitutional rights will you abridge. Mine or these other poor slobs?"

"Do you know what you're getting into?"

"From the tone of your voice, obviously not. But then, if I don't then neither does the community. How is a good time for both of us to find out?"

"Okay, Veauxvois, your wish is granted."

"Stop! Stop! You can't do this! You don't know what you're getting into! You judge, you can't let him do this!" shrieked a young black woman running down the aisle of the courtroom.

"Order in the court! Order in the court!" yelled the crier.

"Who is this woman?" entreated the judge.

"I'm his wife!" yelled the woman.

"Is this your wife, Veauxvois?" the judge asked.

"Well, ah, your honor. Let me have a little conference with her?"

"Is this your wife? Answer me."

"Please your honor. Just a minute."

"Okay. But straighten this out. And I want to know if she's your wife."

"Look, Chris," he whispered to the young woman. "I've got to get in to help the rothers and now is as good a time as any. I may not get another opportunity."

"Those brothers in there have lost their minds, man. They can't see your black soul – they're only gonna see your white skin. They'll do the complete trick on you before they even find out anything about you!" she retorted in a whisper easily heard throughout the courtroom.

"That's just the chance we'll have to take. Remember, I told you it would have to be this way. That it would be those we're trying to help who would inflict all the suffering. That we'd be lucky to live through our good deeds. That's the way it is babe. We didn't create the place. The only thing we can do is try to improve it and hope our deaths aren't too painful."

"Okay, Veauxvois – is she, or isn't she?"

"No, your honor. Just a very dear friend."

"Is that correct, young lady?"

"Yes, your honor."

"All right then, move on. Next case."

Ralph was immediately whisked away into the prison confines immediately behind the courtroom as Chris groped from the courtroom still in tears. Ralph was led into a room where he was required to empty all his valuables, and then placed in a cell containing seven other prisoners, all black except himself. During the remainder of the day, ralph tried unsuccessfully to make friends with the other men. Their animosity toward the man only caused to increase with his friendly statements; therefore, he retreated to his bunk and began to make notes on the pencil and pad he had been allowed to bring into the cell. Aside from a few unkind and crude epithets, nothing much happened for the rest of the day. But then night fell...

"The picnic's over whitey!" a big black man whose life of crime had obviously enhanced his muscular frame. Ralph did not even blink or make recognition of his presence with his eyes.

"You got bad hearin' man? I gonna hep ya fella!"

As he went to grab Ralph by his ears and drag him out of the bunk, Ralph wheeled in his bunk and slammed his heel into the inside of the big man's knee, throwing him quickly off balance onto the floor.

"Sorry, friend," Ralph casually remarked. "didn't realize you were there."

This time is was the big black man's turn for silence – he, however, aimed a vicious look that probably would have killed most men by itself from pure fright.

The result apparently had some effect on the other men. Their formerly uncontrollable attention turned to instant disinterest. Ralph stretched and returned to his bunk to try to sleep through his first night in the infamous Parish Prison of New Orleans, a place so decadent both in its own physical facility and the bottom of the barrel cultural level of the almost unanimous percentage of its inhabitants, who regularly curse passerby, and many of whom make a regular practice of unauthorized leave of the premises. And other things, almost unmentionable things, reported only very occasionally by some culturally middle-classed white student who has the misfortune of no legal pull and a complete absence of judicial compassion, undoubtedly a freak occurrence by a group of judges, who, at the very least, can usually distinguish the relatively cultured and basically harmless "criminal" from the "career (cultureless and therefore very dangerous) criminal."

"Don't you dare move, smart man!" The big black man was sitting on his stomach with a razor at Ralph's throat, two of the other men are sitting on his legs. "Make one sound and it will be your last. You gonna be our woman tonight, white man, or you ain't gonna be here tomorrow."

Ralph starts to struggle, but after a brief wince, he realizes that the razor will make short work of his vocal chords if he should yell, and seven to one odds in the middle of the night are hopeless in a place that is guarded by only two underpaid, poorly trained deputies. The rest might interest the prurient, the anal sex orgy, the sucking, the tit biting – suffice to say that by the end of the night, Ralph did not care if he ever sat again and felt as if he might walk like a gorilla for the rest of his life. It continued for at least three hours in the early morning. First one, then another, then around again – their sexual appetite seemed insatiable. Toward the end, Ralph had begun to groan just a bit; the middle of his body could only be described as raw.

"Come on, Ralph." The voice was Regon's.

"I don't know if I can Ron," Ralph weakly responded. "They gave me the business." The immediate hurt was excruciating, but the thought of more of the same was adequate motivation to drag himself out of the cell.

"The judge knew your reforming zeal would at least suffer a quick taming. You're out on a ROR. We've got a motion to quash set for tomorrow at ten. From what we can tell, there really isn't anything to quash, but it ought to kill the whole thing."

"Anything new on Scotlandville?"

"The governor has ordered an immediate shifting of the juveniles and a reallocation of the funds in accordance with the judgment we had the judge sign late yesterday afternoon. I'm going to take you to the hospital for a check – and you will not insist on being a charity guinea pig this time."

"You just earned an easy win – let's go."

Big Charity, as she is sometimes called, is the largest per bed hospital in the nation whose sole purpose originally was the bring medical care to the poor. She has developed into a great teaching institution, with both the Tulane and LSU medical schools making use of her seemingly insatiable supply of sick by poor economic, living, and working conditions, thereby providing an even greater supply of disease and accident patients than the average private hospital would ever despair having.

A doctor on the emergency staff gave Veauxvois a shot of penicillin after a thorough inspection and sent him on his way.

"Well! Are you satisfied? Did you find what you were looking for? Did they leave anything for me?"

"Not much. And it's awfully bad babe. Seeing you has got me all turned on, and oh how it hurts."

"Suffer, nimblewitt. After those black bastards, I don't know if I ever want you to touch me again. Why in the world do you seem to think that all the guys they lock up are victims of circumstance – believe me, a lot of those guys earned their way in; and many of the rest are no longer any better."

"Okay Chris. Don't act so hurt just because I didn't listen to you the first time or because your pride is hurt."

"You know better than that Ralph! It's your ass that I'm concerned about – and it's not my pride; if that were the case, I wouldn't be here now or ever!"

"I'm sorry. I'm raw in just about every way believable; and like they say in the bible, I mean like The Man said in the Word, when your big toe hurts, you hurt all over. Obviously, it has affected my brain."

A knock on the door interrupted the discussion. When Ralph opened the door, standing there was a skinny little black boy in blue jean cutoffs and a white T-shirt.

"My mama told me they give you the business cause me. She say'd they gonna sen you up the river."

"it's not that bad Fred. Just a bunch of guys who started out like you but never met anybody like me and Chris. They've been dumping on themselves since they were your age – when you've been dumping that long, you tend to get kind of careless and you dump on other people in the process."

"Well, I sure don't wanna dump on you, Mr. Ralph. What kin I do?"

"Is your mama home tonight?"

"No suh, she's workin'."

"What about the other kids?"

"They all sleepin'."

"Well, you stay here tonight with Chris and me. Tomorrow, we're going to make you a TV star."

Tomorrow was not long coming – much too fast for Ralph, and it was quite apparent on his bedraggled face as he, Chris, and Fred walked through the truly impressive old hallway of the Criminal District Court building. Its ancient Greek Renaissance type architecture, marked by extremely high ceilings and large windows almost floor to ceiling, exposing the great Greek columns which adorn the front of the building. The somewhat stark and cold greyish-white marble is a sharp contrast to the warm little group of three promenading rather casually toward a not particularly inviting situation.

The courtroom is not particularly crowded, perhaps half full when the crier announces the entrance of the judge. A parade of individuals to be arraigned is paraded before the judge. In addition to the blue denim inhabitants of Parish Prison, there is a rather large group of individuals who might otherwise appear to be family, except that the difference in race, dress, and natural affinity is quite obviously not present. After dealing with the residents of the nefarious institution located behind the court building, most of them black and most of them charged with victim crimes, and most of them returned to the jail for lack of bond money, a couple bended by attorneys hired by their wives or families.   Then the unlikely group. The old lady who protests her innocence and God-fearing qualities. The young nicely dressed couple with the baby, both on marijuana violations, that victimless crime the judges use to keep their coffers full. The good-looking young man, executive type, charged with obscenity in public that will pay his attorney's bills for that month. A good looking young brown lady in tight pants and halter type blouse, charged with prostitution. None had or would spend any time in the parish detention facilities. Their attorneys would either successfully suppress the evidence against them or they would plead guilty to lesser crimes and pay a nice fine. The fines would keep the courts in business.

These lesser criminals, the amateur criminals so to speak, certainly do not want to make a public issue of their "crimes." They will not have spent any time in the prison so as to be exposed to its outrages and thereby be less inclined to worry about the publicity of their "crimes" and perhaps make known the atrocities perpetrated on the taxpayers, who continue to be assaulted by the economic considerations which actually promote the cycle of crime and prevent the effective use of their tax money to provide the safety for which they pay so much. But then who will tell them that the problem is not what they think it is? Who will admit that most of the drug addicts do not or would not pose any real threat to them (the citizens, the taxpayers) except for the fact that to promote the myth contributes greatly to the soft chairs and long roves of the judges, more patronage and power for the police chief, and more work and a better market for organized crime? Who will tell them that homosexuality is more natural for some people that a heterogeneous relationship is for most, and a better relationship than most, one tempered by the strength that comes only from adversity?   Or that to expect that man's (or woman's or both) oldest profession can be obliterated after all these years all the while ignoring the benefits from tax revenue and medical safety of both the prostitutes and their customers that would be derived from licensing and regulation?

"Evidence of what?   I believe that I was accused of a juvenile delinquent. Lest we waste considerably more time, let me introduce you to this dangerous villain to society."

By this time, Ralph was very impatient. Two hours of listening to the creaking archaic judicial system attempting so unsuccessfully to deal with problems so many of which are either economic and social in origin, or medical in solution, had turned the very casual young lawyer into a disturbed and distraught young citizen. By the time Fred had been "properly" dressed in a suit replacing his tattered jeans, white T-shirt, and holey black tennis shoes.

"Give the court your name, address, and age, please, Fred?"

"Fred Washington, 1708½ Erato St., eleven years old," he answered in his faltering, slurring pronunciation.

"Where have you been hiding, Fred?"

"Nowhere, Mr. Ralph."

"What do you mean, Fred? These people arrested me and put me in with your older "brothers" – and you know what they did to me Fred – because you did something wrong and I helped you get away. Is that true Fred?"

"You know that ain't right, Mr. Ralph. You know it's just like the last ten times I got arrested. When those big guys found out about my thing, they made me do it again, and again, and again – this was just another time."

"What do you mean, Fred? What is you think?"

"Well, you know Mr. Ralph. You know I don't like school, and when I'm not there, I'm hangin' round Joe's mechanic shop, just kinda watchin' and stuff. An' Joe kinda let's me watch a little closer 'cause I help 'im clean sometimes. So I picked up some stuff like how to hot wire a car – that's what they do when they hafta' move the cars around and they're too laze to get the keys; how to break in – same reason; and some other things about what parts are valuable and stuff like that."

"But you must have known it was wrong, Fred."

"Kinda, but what the hell! We didn't have nothin' and we didn't have nothin' to do. The first time was just kinda a joy ride thing. Besides, I got to run with the bigger guys and hump with some older chicks – man, that's fine livin'. An' besides, the rich white dude we borrowed it from probly had a couple others anyway – he sure had a fine chick. I made it to Scotlandville for that one. Met some guys and some more swingin' chicks, and I learned from them more of the marketplace. Afta' a few more busts, I did get a little tired of bein' picked on by the big guys and teased by their chicks, an' my mama locked onto a stud workin' on the docks, makin' good bread so the good was betta' at home. So, the las' time, mama's stud says I got too much talent to be wastin' my time here so he sends me to this place in California where they was a lotta guys like me, mostly older, and a lotta guys like Mr. ralph who really get interested in ya'. I was only there a couple days when Ma said I hada come back 'cause Mr. Ralph been hassled on my count."

BABY SALES

One thousand dollars in ten one hundred-dollar bills is placed carefully, but firmly on his desk along with what appears to be a contract. The prospective new clients appear to be two young women, both pregnant, and a young man, approximately the same age as Veauxvois.

"I believer that I am happy to meet you, but I must admit to being somewhat befuddled as to your calling cards," initiated Veauxvois.

"Why? Mr. Veauxvois? Isn't the first thing a lawyer does is get his fee and make a contract for his employment?"

"Yes, but…"

"Well, there's your fee. The contract says that you will represent Robin Jones-Smith to the highest court in the land if necessary, to obtain his acquittal in the two charges made against him: namely, statutory rape and the sale of minors. The contract stipulates your fees for each level of appeal if necessary. Is there anything else? Oh yes, it contains your processional vow of secrecy with liquidated damages for breach thereof. Is there anything else?"

"I wouldn't think so. But before I take the money and sign the…"

"Are you telling us that it's not enough money?"

"No."

"Well, then, what is the problem?"

"Something about not unfairly taking your money and wasting my time. Tell you what, give me one of those hundred-dollar bills. I'll listen to your side of the story, check it with the court and police record, and then, if I think I can help you, I'll take the other $900 and sign the contract."

After a brief conference, "OK," replied the girl named Holly. "Ill start trying to explain."

"Why not the accused? Doesn't he even know what he's accused of?"

"Not completely. You see, he didn't even make either one of us pregnant, the first time, that is. And he really didn't know I was only fifteen the second time."

"What second time?"

"This time."

"You mean you're fifteen years old and pregnant for the second time already!?!" shrieked Veauxvois, obviously in disbelief.

"Look, Mr. Veauxvois. You don't have to take this case – and besides, you don't have to defend me anyway. It's Robin we want you to defend and he hasn't done anything wrong. We thought you were progressive."

"I thought I was too. But I must admit I have a slight aversion to babies having babies."

"Bonnie and me had the idea. She's three years older, but as I'm sure you noticed, we look very much alike – both blonde, both five foot four, both broad hipped with large vaginas…"

"Broad vaginas!"

"Yes, broad vaginas. Only men with big penises could satisfy us. Like most other girls who are close friends, we compared notes; that's how we know each other so well. That's how when the coach got me pregnant the first time I got pregnant – his penis is as big as a horses'. Man, he felt good. I couldn't get enough of his wang. Hell, the football players used to sneak me in the locker room at lunch cause they knew his wife is frigid and the coach would get unlivable during the season unless he got his ass. Weren't none of them could fill me so that they figured they'd keep all of us happy. Worked well too when the coach broke through his rubbers so often and I got pregnant. Just like we figured his penis much scared his wife frigid, my first baby seemed to warm her back up to the coach. She gladly agreed to play pregnant, I was a little heavy anyway and the baby didn't come till September. My parents – that is, my stepfather and my mother – are always glad to have me gone so they were happy when I spent the whole summer at Bonnie's – her parents were in Europe. Robin came from Vietnam, delivered the baby – he was a Special Forces medic who delivered plenty Montagnard babies – and made the swap for us. We got $5,000 from the coach, his wife got the baby, and we took off. Bonnie's parents is what caused the problem. My mother and the Big Wang – my stepfather was the first one, he's the one who got me started when I was eleven – were glad to see me go. But her parents wanted her to come back, do the society bit at U of T, and marry some oil lawyer from Dallas. That's why the extradition for sale of a baby and statutory rape. That's why Robin married me and not Bonnie who is his real love. She's over eighteen, so she can do what she wants – that's why she let him marry me – naturally, my parents were glad to get rid of me. Anyway, we guess her parents must have set a horde of private investigators on the case. Must figure if they can get Robin put away, we'll have to come back. Well, they're not all right. While Robin can easily keep us pregnant, he can't possibly satisfy us all by himself. But he's got plenty of friends all around who don't wanna get married but need to get the edge off. Some of these guys learned real good from those Vietnamese women – they know how to please us. A few them are real bulls. Anyway, we got plenty of places to go. Her parents are all wet."

"You can say that again, Holly baby!" chimed in the older girl.

"You girls seem awfully chummy? No jealousy? No envy? You almost seem like lovers?" cross-examined Veauxvois in his most sardonic manner.

"We are," both girls stated coldly and flatly in new unison.

"Before Robin came back from Vietnam, there wasn't anybody for us. All the boys in our town were just that – boys. All the men had gone off to war. So, you might say we became lesbians by necessity. We never did find it quite as good as a big good dick, but what's the difference between a man's tongue from a woman's – and our fingers are a lot softer," continued Bonnie.

"Just how does this appeal to you, Robin?"

"Like the lady says, I'm a real stud but I am flesh and blood – these girls are really super women – super nymphos. They really take care of me. I get all the sex I want. Just keep um healthy and happy. When I run out of gas and we're not around any of my friends they can trust and will satisfy em, heck, I even enjoy watchin' em. If a lot more men knew what they know about a woman's body, they'd be a lot less murders. Man, there's heaven between their legs – and they know where it's located."

"So, you people really have sex lives?!"

"Look, Mr. Veauxvois, will you take the case?" requested Holly in a very firm manner, seriously intoned.

"I don't know if I can," joked Veauxvois. The young clients were obviously not amused.

"Do you or don't you take the case?"

"Okay! But…"

"No buts – we have no need of moralistic treatment!" yelled the young girl. "We bring happiness with what we do – who else do you know brings as much happiness as we do for so little."

"Okay, okay."

BAG YOUR TRASH

"Get your tail outa bed, Veauxvois!" intoned the somewhat coarse voice over the telephone near the bed.

"Who in the hell is this, anyway?" muttered Ralph, attempting to clear his brain of sleep.

"Tyronne, man. You remember, we've got to go chasing those garbage trucks this morning."

"What time is it?"

"Four thirty."

"You can't even see now. What in the world can we do?"

"Don't give me all of that crap, man. Roll your ass aw3ay from Chris and get over here."

The New Orleans Jayvees had volunteered to do a study for the City of New Orleans to determine if different types of containerization could improve the efficiency of garbage collection and save the city money while making it cleaner. The study had started with a big ballyhoo intended by certain companies to promote their products and make use of the Jaycee name to give them credence. There was a banquet with a beautiful female professional spokesman telling all the wonderful attributes of her company's plastic bags. It featured an encounter from a representative of the leading ecology group taking the microphone out of the hands of the mayor and denouncing the mayor, the city, and the Jaycees for conducting such a promotion under the guise of a study, and indicating that the study was not necessary. Both the mayor and the Jaycee President made it abundantly clear that what they were doing was only a study and that they would not buckle under from either side. What it made clear was the reason why the mayor had asked the Jaycees to get involved in something that it would otherwise seem would have been a prerogative of his staff:

remove political criticism and scrutiny by involving the strictly impartial Jaycees. After obtaining additional assurances from the mayor's staff, the Jaycees decided that the best way to protect their reputation was to complete the project in their usual objective, thorough, and basic manner; hence, down in the ditches research to dig out the real facts.

Bags supplied by the city had been distributed to residents of the three lowest class, economically, neighborhoods in the city. Two were public housing projects and the other the usual near downtown near alum. Neighborhood Youth Corps participants, kids paid to work on community service projects after school, had done the distribution including an explanation of how the project would work. Tyronne Sims, Jaycee Vice-President in charge of the project and the highest-ranking black man in the New Orleans chapter, had coordinated the distribution through his connections in the black community. He had become a little aggravated by the less than avid attitude of some other Jaycees who seemed somewhat blasé about trying to assist the lower-class neighborhoods with their garbage problems. As a result, he had aroused the Jaycee President (who in every chapter must necessarily be a part of every project) to make the rounds with the garbage men and see if the "new bagging techniques" were really assisting them in speeding up their jobs and making them more efficient.

"I see you've got your trusty camera, Rusty," remarked Ralph. "You gonna take pictures of Tyronne's black ass running through Desire interviewing the garbage men?"

"Your mouth and your mind sure match the subject of this project, Veauxvois."

"Aw, come on Rusty. Tyronne's behind is just perfect for your photography: big and bouncy."

"Man, these guys sure work their butts off. They look to me like they run the whole route. Two cans a crack. Those big paper bags don't seem to make any difference. Looks like a great way to get in shape," mentioned Ralph.

"Well, when they finish a route, they can go on to other jobs. Of course, for most of these guys it just means another route." Tyronne went on to explain that the best pay went to the driver, who, naturally, has the physically easiest job. He then related what a friend of his who was now a missionary had done with this summers during school; that the friend has spent each summer working as a garbage man, getting the job is easy because few aspire to the position, that the men for the most part speak only of sex and money in a vocabulary that would make any avowed curser beam with pride, but that after one route, which would be finished before most people even start for work, he would return home to sleep off his exhaustion.

This offhand little story rang a bell in Ralph's cranium. He had been tiring of his work with NOLAC which had been increasingly hamstrung by the conservative administration in Washington, and he had wanted to make himself available for some criminal appointments, that is, appointments by state criminal court judges to represent indigent criminal defendants for no pay. If Washington did not want him to attack the inadequacies of the system through class actions while being paid to be a lawyer at taxpayer's expense, then perhaps he could do it as a garbage man.

"A what?" queried a startled Sims.

"A garbage man. It'll allow me to get the exercise I need early in the morning and make enough to live in the project and represent some indigent defendants in criminal court while working on some new legislation I have in mind."

"Veauxvois, you must be nuts!" added Rusty. "This place is a jungle. You'll get killed for sure."

"He's right man, you know. It seems all right now because everybody's asleep. But when it wakes up, it's a madhouse."

"Would you believe that's what they told me when I moved into Central City on Baronne Street. It's about time – think I'll give it a try, Chris willing."

And hour or so later back at the apartment on Baronne Street.

"Man, you're some kinda' nut, Ralph! Screamed Chris. "Hey, I want to help my people. But what about this big bulge you so generously donated to my stomach. You want to put this kid in that mess down there? Come on Ralph --- get ahold of your senses!"

"Look, Chris. Would we have even met if I hadn't moved into this so-called Central City mess?"

"Perhaps. Perhaps not. But Central City is not the Desire Project!"

How true. The Desire project is a public housing project built by WPA during the 1930's. It was built on land deemed most undesirable at the time, across the Florida Avenue railroad tracks, in the same direction from downtown New Orleans as the affluent Gentilly area but isolated physically as well as economically from every other part of the city. As definite as the physical isolation is, the economic isolation is considerably crueler. Concisely, the physical setup of Desire is almost identical to the other public housing projects in the New Orleans: concrete three story complexes of approximately twenty four apartments per building, built in a cluster of approximately the same number of buildings as the number of apartments per building. Except for their isolation from the city, the buildings themselves, except for their age perhaps, might very well serve as modern apartment complexes for today's world. The economic isolation makes the big difference: the residents are primarily female, all poor, many aged and very young, few grown males, fewer breadwinners, all black and all poor.

The Black Panthers had almost taken over the project at one time. A confrontation with the police resulted in one of the buildings being blown off the face of the earth. Drug pushers are the most successful businessmen in the area. The police themselves are afraid to enter most projects, but most of all this one.

"Look, Chris. It's going to take some time anyway. I've got to give NOLAC some time to replace me, then see if it's feasible for me to work as a garbage man…"

"Work as a what!?"

"A garbage man."

"No, I know you've flipped. Where in the world did you get that idea?"

"You know, Tyronne's brilliant "Bag Your Trash" survey. That's where we were this morning when I got up at 4:30 am. Just started thinking about how Desire is much like the survey: all the poor black people in the same bag and shoved to the side like garbage. So, how do you improve the situation? Just like you improve bad water: mix it with good water to imp0rove the quality. We did it here in this neighborhood. Why can't we do it there?"

"You've got to remember that there's a lot less isolation here in Central City. For one thing, a lot of people own their own property here and there are very nice neighborhoods nearby. And here, there are all private owners on whom you can put pressure a lot more easily than the housing authority."

"But we're got the law. Ans the law is going to say that they must give us a place there. And the law is going to say they've got to help our neighbors be good ones."

"Where did you get that?"

"It's in the law. It's what the law that set up public housing in the 1930's said the authority is supposed to do. And the 1964 Civil Rights Act says they will have to give us an apartment."

"Gee, I just don't know Ralph. It seems to me you've been helping people at NOLAC. I guess I should be thinking a little more about my own people, especially when you are so willing to do anything to help them. But you do have to think of yourself sometimes. Heck, what point would it be to improve the lot of my people if they wouldn't enjoy it when they got it. It just seems to me that we can help put out the fire without going to live in it."

"Well, let me check out my theories. And then we can go from there. Okay?"

DEAD END ROW

"Are you trying to tell this committee that the Louisiana legislature should give legality to the most mundane and despicable inclinations of man?!"

"Well, your technical analysis is correct – the emphasis lacks. We are not asking you to give respectability to these acts. Only society can do that. What we propose will assure that that will never be the case. We simply suggest that you cannot legalize morality with success – but you can control it!"

"Alright, Mr. Veauxvois. Let us assume that you are correct that there is some value to society in removing the criminal sanctions from the generally accepted vices – but providing them for free at taxpayer's expense! Don't you believe that is going from one extreme to the other?"

"As I pointed out Senator, we are only suggesting a pilot project. It's a simple concept: fight fire with fire, or in this case, fight the evil effects of vice with the evil effects of vice. We're going to let it kill itself. Not only that, we're not asking the legislature to appropriate a nickel. We just want you to pass enabling legislation to allow cities or town or other appropriate political subdivisions to set up the situations. No state tax money."

Back in the NOLAC office.

"It was fantastic! What a show! You should have seen those north Louisiana senators and representatives wailing on the House and Senate floors. I guess it must e toned down from the old days of Huey Long. Ut they still give you a solid dose of that good ole Baptist religion with a dripping redneck drawl. One guy even brought a huge hypodermic needle and a set of stage movies and threatened to strip to the bone until one of the other fellows reminded him that except to the floor of the legislature, he was already guilty of two crimes, possessing pornographic materials with intent to display and possessing narcotic paraphernalia without a license,

and working on a third. But he did make the point for passage – it made
abundantly clear to everyone how illogical most of the present vice laws are.
The bill passed immediately thereafter."

Well, we're home free then," suggested Ron.

"Hell, no!"

"What do you mean?"

"Well, while we may not see too much of that maniacal opposition to
the concept of removing the illegality, squeezing bread out of the City
Council is not easy for any purpose."

"What about the Mayor?"

"Hell, Rob Rucker can't fail to support us! Being the first black mayor
of New Orleans leaves him absolutely no choice. But Rob will support it
anyway. Most of the astute black people have been working in this area for
a long time. Even though most of them would prefer to see the
conventional approach work, they have been considerably more realistic
then our white so-called political leaders."

But in the Mayor's office...

"Look Veauxvois. A lot of my black supporters do understand. But
many will not. Even if they are for decriminalization, they are not for
giving away anything to those who don't need it and would be better off
without it. They are going to be worried that their kids, in the interest of
personal scientific research, are going to give it a try and never come out
alive. Of course, I don't worry about my white supporters because most of
them are kooky white liberals like you. Except our venerable police chief –
but I had to give the rest of the whites something to hang onto.
Remember, he was a narc."

"You don't have to remind me, Mr. Mayor. I keep trying to forget. It
just seems he won't let me."

"Mary, ask Tom McCann to come up, please," requested Mayor Rucker
of his secretary. "Let's find out what approach Tom can suggest. He's
pretty good at these things."

Tom McCann is Mayor Rucker's brother-in-law as well as his chief
administrative officer. Being a white man virtually absorbed in the black
man's world, his professional background included a Harvard master's
degree in business administration and a brief stint at Notre Dame seminary;
his business experience included work with a New York public relations
firm and the largest bank in New Orleans. While at the bank, he had served
as president of the New Orleans Jaycees, a group of young people (not just
men – that's one uproar they were in the middle of) with a very
establishment name, but with many progressive civic credits. As a matter of
fact, some of their inside work had made passage of the "dead End Row"
bill possible; one of the newest members had dreamed up the name. He
had figured that the Baptist hell-fire breathers might go along if it looked

like the thrust was to exhibit a hell on earth.

"Well, Mr. Mayor," responded Tom to the Mayor's request for his opinion. "I understand you used the Jaycees state influence – a mean trick in this case since they've come a long way in this state since my term as president. It seems to be you want to let them loose on the city council."

"Wait a second, Tom!" the mayor intervened. "How are you planning to get past our honorable police chief?"

"She what?!" exclaimed Ralph, incredulously, as in shock.

"She left a note saying that your stupid ideas were finally going to destroy her people, and the least she could do was to save a few of them herself. So, she's signing up to be one of the official prostitutes in one of the brothers there," explained Ron.

Ralph was obviously too surprised and despondent to reply, at first. But after a short while shaking his head, gritting his teeth, and doing a little unidentifiable shrieking, he did make some understandable remarks, "I really thought she understood the whole concept of Dead-End Row. I thought she agreed that it was a good idea to decriminalize the so-called vices and protect the victims by giving them a strong dose they won't forget and then making available to them the necessary medial treatment. I wonder who's been talking to her."

"What are you going to do?"

"I don't know. I guess I'll go down there and see if I can get her to come out."

And so, Ralph headed out of his office to the older part of New Orleans between the central business district and the Industrial Canal, beyond the world-famous Vieux Carre by a few blocks and near the River Front. Three full blocks had been dedicated and expropriated by the city and redeveloped into a mini Las Vegas looking area, officially called "Instant Happiness." Cynics like Ralph knew the truth, the only way a person would come out would be in a pine box.

The whole concept was an extreme attempt to answer a critical problem of drug abuse. Almost every drug store in the city of New Orleans had been subjected to vicious armed robberies in which half of them at least one person was killed. As the police increased their vigilance and became increasingly successful at cutting off the supply of narcotics, the robberies became more frequent and vicious. Because they were never able to cut off the supply completely, addiction flourished, Charity Hospital became flooded with victims of heroin addicts poisoned by substances diluted with rat poison, some, children. And yet, the best that concerned cynics could get the state legislature to allow was a pilot project in the City of New Orleans where the city would actually create an instant nirvana with free dope, free sex (of any sex), and unlimited license to do with yourself whatever you wanted as log as it didn't harm anyone else. Anyone of voting age can enter. The only requirement is that you be a drug addict and that your habit be sufficiently severed to desire at least two fixes a day – there is no upper limit to the theory being that drug addicts are of no value to society anyway, so that if they should die from an overdose then society is ridded of another useless body.

There are no police on the inside; there only function is to control who enters and to protect the employees, such as the registered prostitutes. Anyone in the community submitting proof of addiction can enter, but only once, to encourage maximum use of the facilities, and to assure that a moderate addiction to the pleasures of drugs and sex would be sickening and destructive rather than pleasurable and relaxing. The expectation was that the true sex addicts would kill themselves and that the kids looking for a thrill would learn a lesson they would never forget and impart that lesson to many of their friends.

Preliminary reports had showed that the incident of armed robberies and killings had almost ceased to exist, much to the chagrin of the police department which had predicted that the project would only create new addicts from people who would not otherwise have become subjected to it. But the statistics had also shown that the percentage of dead being removed were largely black, and under twenty-five and male.

"Look, this whole project was my idea. You've got to let me in. There's a girl in here who doesn't belong. Just give me an hour," leaded Ralph to the policeman at the admitting station.

"So, you're the genius. Well, genius, they all have the same story. There little boy or little girl doesn't know what she's gotten into. Sorry chump. Show me proof of addiction, and you can have your shot at instant happiness. Otherwise, I suggest you head for church and pray for your little bird."

Ralph walked off dejectedly. He had tried many things in his time, but he had never been able to dig with any regularity even a passing drinking habit. So, he did just what the man suggested, he headed for church to hope and pray for Chris.

Meanwhile, inside, Chris was getting acquainted with Instant Happiness. Physically the place was a real showplace. It was hygienically clean. Even the streets outside seemed to be as sanitary as a hospital. The architecture appeared to be straight out of Disneyland. All the old buildings had been completely renovated and even some modern ones had been added to make everyone happy. The sound of beat music could be heard drifting through the streets and the aroma of booze and hashish filled the air. The only strange thing was that there are few places to eat because addicts generally aren't too interested in food.

Inside the brothel entitled "Marie Le Veau" Chris heard from the Madam, an experienced black hooker who had been hired to run one of the two integrated (in terms of available female flesh) houses, some of the techniques that were expected to be used. The décor of the building was turn of the century, in keeping with the actual age of the building, although the building had probably never seen days so prosperous with expensive chandeliers, rich carpeting, and red velvet wallpaper.

"I'm sure you all realize and have looked forward to this assignment with great pleasure, knowing that you will be experiencing the most extreme forms of sexual interaction," the madam explained. "Your job is to assure that our clients experience the broadest and most far-flung amount of pleasure in extreme doses. Remember that in addition to your extremely good salaries (I'm sure a few doctors and lawyers wish they had the bodies to sign on) you'll get a $5,000 bonus for every dude you handle who leaves your room and leaves here directly, and it doesn't matter whether it's in a box or on his own two feet."

Chris, appalled at the obvious intent to have the dope addicts murder themselves with excessive doses of drugs, asked, "Why $5,000?"

"The City Council and state legislature figured that was a bargain because it costs the city and state at least that much to maintain one of the guys in prison for one year, and they would probably occupy that place for a few years. Any other questions?"

Chris and the other girls were then each shown their rooms. Each one was luxuriously appointed with its own dual bathing facilities and the bell for instant room service, to refill the exquisite decanters of drugs carefully and attractively labeled, readily available on a bureau much like cigarettes or booze or candy sticks. As a matter of fact, there were some candy sticks containing LSD and pure heroin among other things.

After being fitted for her gowns, designed to show the bestial sexual quality of the women and personalized to highlight the best physical qualities of each, the girls were to return and begin work. Although "Instant Happiness" is open 24 hours a day, most of its clients only appear after ten or eleven o'clock at night. So, it was for Chris' first night at work.

She was down in the exquisite parlor with the large gold gilded mirror and blood red drapes, when a young black man in tennis shoes without socks, khaki pants showing the signs of no care and work, and a torn white T-shirt arrived. After sampling the available girls mainly by touch, in his case by physically feeling the crotch of the three girls who were available, he shrieked with delight when Chris screamed as he was barely able to get his finger inside of her. She quickly recovered her composure and smiled, "Oh, that was good. If you cock is half as good as your finger, I'm going to love this."

"You're not jiving me, are you sweet mama?"

She stuck her hand in his pants and grabbed his balls with such speed that he nearly jumped though the ceiling. "Come on, baby. I can see those tattered old clothes are hiding a real man under there."

Surprised and tamed by her unexpected aggressiveness, the two of them exited up the stairs to her room, where she unclothed him and fitted him with a velvet robe and slippers. At first he started to try to rape her, but when she pointed out that he could have all he wanted of her and the candy jars and she quickly beat him off with her hand, he because like a pussycat in a lions den. Even with her admonitions to take it easy if he wanted to be around at least a little while to enjoy it, she still had to serve him some beer and barbs and light him a joint, which adequately calmed him, to allow her to convince him to take a bath with her. Even more coaxing to let her clean him up and not ruin the place for the all-night sex and drug orgy they were about to have all night, and into the days until he wanted to quit.

RETIREMENT OF THE HIPPIE LAWYER

"He what?" questioned the astonished Mayor of New Orleans.

"He announced his retirement," repeated the Mayor's personal secretary.

"That man must have lost his mind! He can't do that. We've been counting on him to bridge the gap in this city. I really expected him to be the next important political force in this city. I just can't understand. Would you try to get him on the phone please?"

"Yes sir."

A little later.

"I can't reach him, sir. His house phone doesn't answer, and he hasn't been in to work at the sanitation department in the last two days."

"Unbelievable! To think… Look, get Max to go over to his apartment to see if he can find him. Tell him to find out whatever he can."

A few hours later.

"The authority says he let his apartment lease lapse. The neighbors say he and his wife just packed the old Volkswagen bus, said their goodbyes, and left. Ron over at NOLAC says he had been by their office a couple of days ago to say goodbye. Said they had bought an old farm in Vermont where the price land is restricted, and he got a nice little farm on his G.I. bill. Said something about doing something productive for a change. Said he wanted to get in a little of the other part of his life now. Something about the good part of his life."

"What about Chris?"

"Not a word except that she went with him."

"I just can't understand it. Chris has always prodded him about contributing and making the city a better place to live. She knew what he could and had to do. Get Ron at NOLAC on the phone for me."

"Well, Mr. Mayor, Ralph often said cramming all of these people together in one place was a hell of a place to live. But when he also always said he might get awfully bored without all the people. He used to tell me that New Orleans was almost ideal as a place to live because it has most of the bennys of a big city with the lifestyle of a small town. But I know he was never satisfied just practicing law. That's why he took that job with the Sanitation Department."

"I know all of that Ron. But I always got the impression that he felt a commitment to the poor people of this city, that he could see this city as having the potential to give the most balanced lifestyle to all of the people, black and white, all races, all religions."

"That's true Mr. Mayor, but he was tired too. I was at his apartment last weekend. He had finally succeeded in having the Housing Authority establish a plan to have the Desire Project, as a pilot project, set up in a condominium situation, allowing middle class families to move in a governed by a resident board to directors. He said he knew there would always be problems, he knew of many more he wanted to work on, but by the same token he was tired, tired of the constant fighting with those he felt should be working with him. Tired of the constant battle with those he was trying to help. He seemed to feel that a breakup of the whole public housing system so that all the poor would no longer be crowded together was kind of a pinnacle. He just felt that he needed some peace and quiet, some real back to nature stuff."

"But what about Chris? How could she let him leave the problems of her people? It just doesn't seem like her."

"Come now, Mr. Mayor. You must know about the real human race. I know you know. I can only answer you by saying the sparkle in her eyes when he told the few of us at his apartment what they were planning to do. It was as clear as day; she a woman first, and a black woman second. She hasn't seen much of him since the baby was born. You could see she was really relishing the thought of their spending all of their time together."

"Amen, Ron. Amen. He's even smarter than I thought. He retired while he can still enjoy it. He can work later, when he's too old to enjoy life."

"Right on, Mr. Mayor. Please let me know if there's anything else I can do for you."

THE HIPPIE LAWYER: THE END OR THE BEGINNING?

"Ok Ralph! So, you think you can enter the race at this point and still even have a snowball's chance in hell of getting recognized much less winning the office of president of the United States?"

"I don't know but since I never approach anything that way, I figure I have nothing to lose," responded the still spry 60-year-old former U.S Congressman and Senator. "All I know is that I have a reasonable shot at being in the running in enough states to win enough votes as a true independent to throw the race into the house of representatives where anything can happen especially right now. We've created a coalition of equally independent former Congress persons and senators around the country who are concerned that the two major parties have run off the rails leaving the middle wide open for a candidate and ticket which will reflect the will of a majority of the electorate which now is in fact majority independent and does not have an allegiance to any party."

"My gosh, Ralph! I think you've been drinking some of the 'jungle juice' the president produces based on how he wondrously arose to the White House."

"I can see that but a similar attempt was made about 10 years ago to create a ticket representing both parties which might well have succeeded except that the mechanism to promote the choice of the candidates simply didn't complete the necessary process adequately to include enough participants. I believe we can do that today with the social media the president so frequently misuses."

"And how do you propose to overcome his massive advantage and that of the 'evil Dems' as he calls them.

"It's actually quite simple. We are enrolled in every state under a placeholder which will permit us to provide a national ticket in enough time, say two or three months prior to the presidential election. Then we avoid attacking the others but simply provide an easily identifiable platform which most of the population wants and show how it can easily be implemented. No matter how vigorously it or we are attacked or opposed, we simply make it clear that we promise to implement it immediately upon being elected. Since we will probably not be considered viable, we can run under the radar until when the votes are counted, they find that we have won enough electors to throw the race into the House of Representative where I believe my record of even handed honesty and significant accomplishment will wipe out the incessant rancor between the two major parties and permit the house to choose us to bring sanity back to the county!"

"Seems very Pollyan-ish to me!"

"You're probably right but in the Mary Poppins school of management and politics, anything is possible. If you would have told me 35 years ago that the current president could be elected, I would have convulsed laughing. And despite the current dark comedy he rules over, he deserves credit for proving that anyone, no matter how qualified, no matter how much baggage, can win. The trick we think is to be able to show the comparisons of what is and what can easily be, and we are on our way! Besides, we have nothing to lose and the citizens have everything to gain."

"God bless you Ralph and the United States of America!